SNAKE MOON

Other books by Ray Manzarek:

The Poet in Exile
Light My Fire

SNAKE MOON

A NOVEL BY

RAY MANZAREK

Based on an unproduced screenplay by
Rick Valentine and Ray Manzarek

NIGHT SHADE BOOKS
SAN FRANCISCO & PORTLAND

First Edition

ISBN-10
1-59780-041-4 (Trade Hardcover)
1-59780-042-2 (Limited Edition)

Night Shade Books
http://www.nightshadebooks.com

ONE

It was a full moon in Taurus, the best night of the year for planting. The moon always came to its fullness somewhere between mid-April and mid-May, and it was then that the earth was ready. Ready to receive the seeds of the tillers of the soil, deep into herself, into her hidden places. It was the full moon after the spring equinox and it was the beginning of the time of potency.

Boone knew this and he had prepared for it. Six months ago he had buried cow horns that he had filled with their droppings. They had cured and tempered and were then ready to mix with water. Boone had used a stick to swirl the buckets of pure rainwater in a clockwise direction, making a whirlpool in each bucket as he poured the cured manure into the vortex. He had continued to swirl the vortex for a minute or so and then rotated the stick in a counterclockwise direction against the energy, creating a chaos not unlike the primordial chaos before creation, and then he swirled it clockwise again until another precise vortex formed, whirlpooling itself to the bottom of the five gallon buckets he used. He had done this for an hour with each bucket.

The fluid that resulted from all this intensity was known as golden water. A man could get anything to grow using that light golden liquid, especially on the night of the full moon in Taurus.

Boone had his seeds with him that night and he was going to sprinkle the golden water over his field and especially over each seed that he placed in the freshly tilled ground. He knew there was a kind of magic to the clockwise swirling of the water and the creation of the vortex and the six months burial of the horns, but he didn't understand it. He did as his mother had done and her mother had done and perhaps all the Dillard women had done back to the time of the Druids. For it seemed to Boone that this ritual was of an ancient origin, having something to do with the rotation of the Earth and the energy that revolved within the Earth and came up to the surface at different points on the globe. Power points like the mounds and serpent shapes that he had seen over in the next county when he went on a journey a few years ago. They were built by the Indians a long time before any white men had ever come to America, and no one alive today knew who made them or what they meant.

But Boone knew they related to the energy. The energy that sustained and supported all life. And Boone also knew that he was living in harmony with the energy. For his life in the little hollow of Coker Creek—with his wife Cassandra and his son Chap and the new baby, his sister Jewel and her husband Jebber, and his grandmother Delilah—was about as close to perfect as a life could be. They had everything they needed and not too much of anything. They worked hard, the land was good, and their Heavenly Father rewarded them. They were happy, they were young, and they were alive in the year of our Lord of 1863.

And that night, under the full moon of Taurus, Boone would begin to plant his crops.

He usually worked the fields with Jebber and sometimes with their wives, but on a night like this he wanted to be alone with his land. He wanted to stand in the middle of the field, barefoot, and feel the earth on his feet. He had taken off his shoes and stood quietly with his toes dug into the soft, Tennessee soil. His soil. And the soil had a warmth to it, a nurturing warmth that seemed to Boone to come from the core of fire at the center of the Earth. The warmth seemed to radiate upward from that molten mass of hellish brimstone that acted as a liquid center-of-balance for the rotation of the planet as it coursed through its arc around the sun. That terrible fire gentled itself as it rose to the surface until it was at the right temperature to sustain life and nurture all the destinies that played themselves out on the skin of Mother Earth.

Boone had been looking forward to this night. He had wanted this moment of peace with his little parcel of land. He had wanted to talk to his land as he had done before on the solstices, when the sun was at its highest and lowest points in the sky. On those days he would take his son with him and they would stand in the middle of the field—the cold and barren field if it was the winter solstice—and Boone would tell the earth that it did not have to worry any longer, the sun was coming back, it would not go any lower in the sky and the light from above would soon increase, warming everything. And Boone felt that the earth took consolation in that knowledge, that it needed to be reassured by its humans that the cycle would again repeat itself and the sun would not just go lower and lower in the sky until it finally disappeared. And, in a way, Boone needed to reassure himself and his son of the same thing.

At the summer solstice, when the sun reached its highest point in the sky, Boone and his son would tell the earth to prepare itself for the heat that was to come. And also to pray for rain during the heat of summer lest everything burn in the fires of Armageddon. And the earth understood and was happy that Boone and his son would tell it these things. Of course, Boone knew that the earth already knew everything but he felt that his conversations with the mother were necessary for the continued happiness of all three of them. It was good for a man and his son to talk to their mother, and the earth was the mother of all things. And he knew that the earth wanted to be included in the lives of her children. So he talked to her, and she responded to him and his family with good harvests and healthy animals and fine children there in Coker Creek Hollow. And it was almost paradise.

The night of the full moon in Taurus was different from the solstices, though. It was the night of secrets and sex. It was the night of special ripeness when Boone would drop his seeds into the soil and add the golden water to the seeds and the mystery of germination would begin. The mystery of life and creation. Only the earth knew how life was created and it was her secret. And it was called sex.

Boone looked forward to that night. He looked forward to being with the earth under the fulgent light of the moon. And he especially looked forward to being soft and warm with the soil and whispering to it about the secrets of life. Like a lover.

But something felt different that night. The light from the moon was not quite right. It was as if something was binding the silver, somehow holding back the full glow of the sun's reflection off that lunar sphere. Boone felt a slight chill in his body even though it was a fine and warm night. He looked up into the canopy of diamonds over his head and saw that the moon was encircled by a cloud. A thin cloud that seemed to wrap itself three or four times around the lady of the night. Girdling her and restricting her light. But there were no other clouds in the night sky. It was clear as could be and the heavens opened themselves into infinity. Boone saw thousands and thousands of stars, twinkling and dancing in the blackness of that limitless space. He knew some of the brighter ones were planets and he knew some of the clusters corresponded to the signs of the zodiac. But he didn't know which stars were which signs. He had read once that the ancient Greeks saw all kinds of animals and gods in the star patterns, and he remembered a dark mass called the Horse Head Nebula in Orion and the strange constellation of Bernice's Hair and something terrible called the Ghoul's Head Nebula in Scorpios. But he didn't know where they were and he didn't *want* to know where such things were. But he did know that he was standing under a full moon in Taurus. And something didn't feel right.

Then he remembered his grandmother Delilah saying something about a snake moon. A moon that was a sign of change, and not for the better.

She had told him of one when he was only ten years old and within a month's time his grandfather had died of a bad snakebite and his grandmother had wept for an entire month for the loss of her man. As far as Boone knew they had been together forever and the tragedy and the weeping had more or less silenced her from that point on. She told things to Boone only reluctantly and only when they seemed to him to have a great weight and importance. Things like the rotation of the energy around the planet, and the burying of the cow horns, and the creation of the vortex in the pail of water. She shared her knowledge of the earth with him, but only on her terms and only in her time. And consequently Boone listened carefully to everything she had to say. Especially when they concerned things that weren't talked about in the weathered Bible that rested on a small table in his house.

And a snake moon was never talked about in the Bible, but

there was Boone standing under one on the night of the full moon in Taurus. He felt a chill rush across his spine and his nerve ends shivered into alertness. He should have been dropping his seeds into the ground but he stood motionless, staring ahead at the forest just beyond the field. He felt as if there was something at the edge of the green wall, waiting for him to come to it. And then he saw a movement a few feet back into the green, the virtually impenetrable green where the wildness lived. Where the Indians once lived and where the creatures of the night lived. He couldn't be sure what it was or even if he had seen anything at all, but his nerve ends sent a cold electrical spark through him telling him that something was in fact there. He put down his seed bag beside his pails of liquid and began to walk through his field toward the forest edge, as if in a dream.

The moon illuminated everything around Boone in a tallow wash. It was usually a silver radiance on the night of a full moon but this snake moon had sucked all the brilliance out of the light and was casting a strange, waxen yellow over the earth. A waxen yellow not unlike his grandmother's ancient flesh and not unlike the flesh of a corpse. As Boone neared the almost black-green wall of the forest he could feel the temperature falling with each step. The green wall seemed to be pulling the warmth out of the field—drawing the life out of everything in the clearing—creating a vacuum in time. Boone trembled in the approaching void, unsure of who, or what, was in the green.

Then he saw a rustle of branches and it stopped him cold. "Who's there," he called out into the night air. There was no answer. But the rustling abruptly stopped and Boone didn't know if it was a varmint, or a bear, or something else. Or if he had seen anything at all.

And then, somehow, he was at the edge of the field. Another step would take him into the labyrinth of the wildness, but he would not take that step. Not tonight. Normally he loved the forest, he loved its freedom and its uncontrolled tangle of life. But tonight it was cold and foreboding, and he would not go into it. As he stood before its immensity, peering into it, trying to see if anything was really there, a mist seeped out of the forest, slowly and silently. It crawled up to him and then it began to encircle him. It was like an ordinary ground fog that he had seen hundreds of times except that this mist began to creep up

Boone's body, moving around his feet, up his legs, covering his thighs, then his groin, then his chest and lungs, restricting his breath, and finally encircling his head and entering his mouth and nostrils. He stood almost unable to move, enveloped by the mist. Encircled like the moon itself. He had become like the snake moon.

And then a voice called out to him. A woman's voice. And it came from within the green.

"Boone. I'm waiting for you, Boone."

It was soft and sweet. Just a delicate whisper in his ears, but yet a voice of sorrow and mournfulness. There was an ice in that call, a frozen note that sounded the tone of the grave. Boone shuddered in the mist that encircled him. He peered into the forest, eyes wide with apprehension, but there was nothing to be seen. Only the impenetrable black-green. The vacuum in time had stopped everything. The moment seemed frozen in space and Boone could not move. The ice in the woman's voice had petrified him and he felt a dread enter his heart; a terrible dread that closed over all the love and warmth that emanated from that energy center in his chest. And he began to feel lost. And terrified.

Then the woman's voice came again. "Oh, Boone. I'm waiting for you. I'm waiting for you, Boone."

But this time there was a sweet, bell-like tone to the voice and the ice was shattered. Like a thin sheet over a pond upon which a rock is dropped, the ice broke into a thousand pieces and the water below was allowed to flow free. So the liquid in Boone began to again flow free and the fear began to retreat from him even as the mist that encircled him began to retreat back into the forest. The tone of the woman's voice had lost its awful chill and the spell had been broken.

Boone took a deep breath and filled himself with the heat of his spirit. His courage came back to him and he found his voice.

"Who's there?" he said again. "Is anyone there?"

There was another rustle in the green and Boone thought he saw the shape of a young woman moving back into the darkness. He shuddered again, struck with the thought that there might actually be someone in there, and called out, "Miss, wait!" The rustling stopped and what he thought might have been a figure seemed not to be there at all. Boone peered hard into the green and called out one last time, "Is anyone there?" There was no answer.

There was only the snake moon.

TWO

The morning came clear and beaming. It was spring in Coker Creek Hollow and life was at its full rush of return. There was no trace of the snake moon, the mist, or any apparition. The earth had exploded with joy in the rich dawning sunlight. The birds were busy about their chores of singing and nest building, the trees had come full and green, the apple and cherry and pear trees had set their flowers and were calling to the bees in the valley to make love to them. As were all the meadow flowers of that bit of Eden in the southeastern corner of Tennessee.

A batch of piglets had popped into the world and the sow was lying easy on her side, nursing her little pig brood. The milk cow was fat and full of fresh greens, the tender and succulent greens of the spring grass after a winter of dry hay. The chickens were busily pecking at the earth and working the underbrush for as many fresh new insects as they could find and devour. And the insects were especially good that year, ripe with delicious juices hidden beneath their crisp exteriors. The flying insects were softer than the crawling bugs, but the softest of all were the worms, and they just might have been the chicken's favorites. But this spring, with all the buzzing, scurrying, wiggling, and burrowing of the reborn insect world, the chickens were in heaven. As was everything in Coker Creek Hollow.

Cassy had risen early with the first light of dawn and was busy in the kitchen stoking the fire and preparing a big breakfast for Boone and Chap. She knew they needed a good start, for Boone and Jebber and Chap were going to kill a pig today. One of last year's brood that had been out working the mast on the forest floor, the acorns and the chestnuts and the mushrooms, and had now reached its full size yet still retained the sweetness and the softness of a yearling. Just the right age to give up its life for the continued life of the family. And this was to be a special killing, too, for it was the first time that Chap would be allowed to actually cut the animal's throat. Cassy also knew that Boone had worked long and hard into the heart of the night, sowing his seeds under the full moon in Taurus. Or so she thought.

So she prepared her excellent buttermilk biscuits and would serve them with some fresh butter that her mother-in-law Delilah had churned the day before. Some of the good, new spring butter from the grass-fattened milk cow. And in her mind's eye, Cassy could see the old woman sitting before the big five-gallon stoneware butter churn and singing an endless chant to herself to set a rhythm on the upstroke and the downstroke of the dasher rod:

"Come butter come
Come butter come
Peter standing at the gate,
Waiting for a butter cake.
Come butter come."

And Cassy had to smile to herself at the old woman's song, for Delilah rarely spoke and to hear her actually singing brought a joy to Cassy's heart. The old woman was a trove of knowledge but would share it with Cassy only infrequently and only in the most important of situations. But she was a good woman and Cassy knew there had been a great tragedy in her life that had silenced her, but she'd never have dreamed of asking Delilah to speak of it. That would be terribly impolite and far too personal for a young woman to ask of her mother-in-law. Although she felt that Boone knew, Cassy never could bring herself to ask him about it, either. But she loved the old woman and respected her dignity and her connection to the earth. And to the Earth Mother. For Delilah seemed as old as the hills themselves.

And so Cassy worked on her biscuits, kneading them and shaping them, slicing up the last of the bacon nice and thick the way Boone liked it, and starting up a pot of coffee, dark and strong, also the way Boone liked it. She popped the biscuits into the oven and went out to the chicken coop to gather up a basket of fresh eggs from the hunter-forager chickens. But before she could step into the home of her little beasts, she heard some suspicious grunting coming from Jebber and Jewel's cabin, which was only a few yards from the chicken coop. Cassy stopped and then smiled in recognition. It was spring and she knew what they were up to. And feeling a bit devilish, she moved softly to the cabin to take a peek. She looked in through the corner of the window, being careful to hide herself as best she could, and sure enough there they were, on the bed, naked as the day they were born. Jewel was on her hands and knees and Jebber was behind her, bent over her and riding her like a hog. He was grunting and snorting and thrusting like a young bull and Jewel was receiving each thrust with a squeal of delight. Her eyes were closed and her head was bobbing up and down in rhythm with her husband's thrusts. And then, as their rhythm continued, she reared her head back, seemed to pause for a moment, and then let out a cry of ecstasy as her passion took over her entire body and she came to her climax. And Jebber just kept thrusting and grunting until he, too, let out his cry of delight. And then they collapsed. Jewel could no longer take his weight and fell face first onto the bed and Jebber fell with her, laughing and howling with delight. And then Jewel laughed and squealed and rolled over to face her man. She embraced him, wrapped her legs around him, and kissed him long and hard on the mouth. Then she reached down between Jebber's legs and guided him back into her. They were going to do it again.

Cassy was transfixed by their lovemaking. Her mouth was slightly open and she was breathing hard. In time with them. In time with their rhythm. And a desire began to rise up in her. She felt a great longing for Boone deep within herself, for she hadn't made love to him since the baby was born. She had tried her best to satisfy him with her hand but she hadn't had him inside of her. And now she wanted him. The baby was four months old and now it was time for her to take her man into her just as Jewel was doing.

Cassy backed away from the window in a heated mist of desire and walked dreamily to her chicken coop. She hadn't felt such stirrings in herself for a long time now. And she liked it. She liked the flushed warmth that seemed to spread over her entire body. And she liked the wetness she felt inside of her, where she would receive Boone, taking him deeply into herself. She loved Boone's hardness. It had made a woman of her. She had never had a man before Boone and he had made the great shiver of ecstasy spread through her entire body. She knew she had become a woman with his hardness inside of her and her arms and legs coiled around him like a snake and the electricity surging and coursing through her body as she surrendered herself to a pleasure she had never before known. It had swept her away and she knew that she would love Boone forever. He was her man and everything that she was as a woman belonged to him.

As she gathered the fresh eggs from her chickens, the Rhode Island Reds and her Buff Cochins and her Leghorns with their bright red combs, she thought she just might creep back into bed with Boone and have him take her that very morning. And the thought of that abandonment to desire made her smile and she began to hum a little song to herself. But as the eggs filled her little basket, their weight brought back the weight of reality and Cassy knew there would be no lovemaking that morning. There was simply too much to do, for today was the day the men were going to kill a pig. And they needed a good breakfast and the baby needed his milk, and the milk cow needed milking, and everything had to be made ready for the butchering of the hog, and Chap was going to do the killing, and the smokehouse had to have its fire going for the hams and shoulders and the middlin' meat that would become their sweet country bacon, and the boiling water had to be gotten ready to scald the pig so its hairs and bristles could be scraped clean and…well, there was just too much to do. There was just too much life on her farm and Cassy smiled again to herself, but this time with the knowledge that it was, indeed, *her* farm. And she loved it. She loved her farm and she loved her life with her family, and tonight she would make love to her husband.

Delilah, who had a little room out back, was up and sitting on the porch, fingers busily working on her knitting, as Cassy came back with the morning eggs.

"You're up early, Grandma," Cassy said.

"I thought I heard some pigs ruttin' and squealin'. Darn if they didn't wake me up. Then I realized it warn't pigs." And Delilah smiled knowingly at Cassy. "You didn't maybe see those pigs, did you girl?"

Cassy blushed. Delilah knew everything and this fine spring morning had even loosened her tongue.

"How'd you know, Grandma?"

Delilah cackled. "It's spring, ain't it? I remember what it feels like. How good it feels. And I remember Lem inside of me. I remember holdin' him and cryin' out for the joy of bein' alive." And her eyes grew moist in the thought of her youth and her long-passed husband. She became silent and tears began to trickle down her cheek.

"Oh, Grandma…" Cassy said in sympathy.

But Delilah was lost in the memory of her time as a young woman on the Dillard farm. Her farm that was now Cassy's farm. And then the memory went away and Delilah wiped her eyes, staring straight out ahead of her, as if she were seeing something in the distance. Something yet to come.

"You'd better hold that man of yours, Cassy. He's restless. I can feel it. He's got the wanderin' in him."

She looked up at Cassy, into her eyes. And Cassy saw into the deep wells of wisdom from which Delilah viewed the world. And she saw the knowledge in the old woman, and was in awe of it.

"You make love to him, you hear me? 'Cause somethin's comin' and I don't like the feel of it."

Cassy became afraid. "What is it, Grandma?"

"I don't know, girl. Just love him, that's all. He needs it…and so do you."

And then Delilah laughed, breaking the spell of the moment. "Good Lord, don't pay any attention to me. I'm just an old woman with a head full of memories." She swiped at Cassy, giving her a slap on the butt. "You go fry up those eggs, my love. Us Dillards got ourselves a big day. It's pig killin' today and Chap's goin' to take his first step into manhood." She swiped out again, "Now git, girl!"

Cassy, unnerved, stepped into the little house with her basket of fresh eggs and the cloud immediately lifted from her. There was Chap, already awake, rocking the baby's cradle. It delighted Cassy's heart to see her two sons together. They're like angels of the dawn, she thought, all pure and sweet and innocent.

"He woke up and started to cry, Ma. I didn't want him to wake Pa so I just got up and talked to him and started rockin' him and he just fell back asleep."

She smiled. "You did good, Chap. You have to look after your little brother 'cause you're the big, strong one. An' he's your blood kin."

"He sure is small."

"So were you, Chap. You were just like him."

"Well, I ain't small no more, Ma. I'm gonna kill a pig today!" Chap proudly said.

"I know you are, sweetheart."

Chap was nearly bursting with excitement. "I'm goin' out with Pa and Jebber and we're gonna get a yearling hog and we're gonna kill it and I get to cut its throat."

Cassy beamed at her little warrior. "I'm gonna fry up a big batch of eggs and some bacon and I got biscuits workin' in the oven, too. And Grandma churned up some fresh butter yesterday."

"I think the smell of them biscuits is what woke me up, Ma." He laughed. "Maybe the baby, too. I'll bet he's hungry for some biscuits. And some eggs, too!"

Cassy's heart filled with love at the sweetness of her boy's laughter. She thought it must surely be the way angels in Heaven sound when they talk to each other.

"I don't know that he's ready for biscuits and eggs quite yet, sweetheart."

"But I bet he'd like 'em, Ma. I sure do!"

"And you're gonna need plenty of fuel for your work today. And so is your father. You go wake him, now. I'll take care of the baby."

Chap stood up from the cradle. "What we gonna name him, Ma?"

"I'm not sure yet, Chap. I thought of calling him Lemuel, after Grandma's husband. But I'm not sure if she'd even want that, to be reminded of things like that."

"Things like what, Ma?"

Cassy paused for a second, thinking about what Delilah had said on the porch. "Things that she lost."

Cassy set the little basket of eggs on the table and bent over the crib to pick up the quietly sleeping baby. "But I'm partial to Luke or Matthew."

"When do we decide?"

"When we baptize him."

"When's that gonna be?"

"When the preacher comes."

"When's that, Ma?"

"I don't know, Chap. We ain't seen him since last fall, but I reckon he'll be by now that spring's come. We'll just have to wait till then."

Cassy held the baby in her arms, opened her blouse, and rubbed his little mouth against her full and rounded breast. The baby woke and immediately took her nipple. He made little cooing sounds, like a dove, as he drew his mother's rich milk down into his hungry belly. Cassy smiled and stroked his back.

"But Ma, what if the baby should die before he has a name? Will he git to go to Heaven? Will they let him in if he don't have a name?"

"Chap, what a thing to say. Of course they will. The angels would just welcome this little soul with open arms. He's one of them. And so are you, Chap. Now you go wake your father and don't be thinkin' about the baby dyin' or nothin' like that. You hear me?"

Chap hung his head contritely. "Yes, Ma."

"Now, git," Cassy said half-seriously and half in jest.

Chap shuffled off into the bedroom and Cassy began her one-handed breakfast preparations, the baby held against her hip and firmly attached to her nipple. With her free right hand she opened the oven door and took out the golden buttermilk biscuits. Their smell filled the kitchen with what Cassy thought must be the way Heaven smells. Rich, warm, and buttery.

Cassy smiled and spoke softly to her little baby. "This is going to be a very good day," she said.

THREE

Jebber and Jewel slowly rolled out of bed, their strong, young bodies glistening with sweat. They had only been married for eight months and the flame of new passion kept them going at each other in every spare moment. Jebber stretched himself in the morning light. He was a handsome young man with dark, curly hair, a strong jaw, an aquiline nose, deep brown eyes that had a wild flash and glint to them, and strong, sinuous muscles that rippled over his entire body. He was a fine specimen. The only thing wrong with him was that he had the mind of an eight-year-old.

When he was just a babe, a yellow stoneware pitcher had fallen off a shelf above his crib and hit Jebber a glancing blow on the back of the head. It didn't even draw blood but it was just enough to leave some kind of permanent damage in his brainpan that made him an idiot. Or rather, a funny, rascally, petulant, exuberant boy in a man's body. And everyone in the family loved him. And Jewel, of course, most of all. She had first been taken by the flash in his eyes, captured by what she thought was a kind of vague wildness in Jebber, a sort of poetic wildness which she later discovered actually turned out to be a little boy's unbridled joy of life. But by then it was too late, for Jewel had fallen in love with Jebber. And they were married by the itinerant preacher the last time he had passed through Coker Creek Hollow. And they were deliriously happy with each other. Jebber was twenty-three and Jewel was nineteen. And they were Mr. and Mrs. Jebber Stubbs.

Jewel rustled up a fine breakfast of hot cakes, bacon, and coffee for the two of them. Jebber had a big glass of milk because he did not like the bitter taste of coffee. But he did like the sweet cane syrup that Cassy had made and he poured it over everything on his plate.

"We're gonna kill a pig today, Jewel," Jebber said as he ravenously ate his breakfast.

"I know, lover. I know you are."

"And Chap's gonna kill it."

"I know."

"I wisht I could kill it."

"But it's time for Chap to learn to do it."

"I'm good at it. I can kill good."

"I know you can, but Chap's got to learn, too."

"I know he does, just like I did. And I can kill good now, too. Hell, I can kill better than Boone. He always stops before he cuts. Like he's scared or sumpin'."

"I don't think he's scared, Jebber."

"He *is*. But I ain't. I just cut 'em right 'cross the throat and they's dead. It don't hurt 'em none." He took a big gulp of his milk, washing down his syrup-smothered breakfast.

Jewel patted her husband's hand. "You're a good man, Jebber."

"I wouldn't want nothin' to be hurt. 'Cept if it was a poison snake, or sumpin'. Then I'd kill it."

Jewel lazily finished her breakfast and sipped her coffee. "I once heard my grandma talk about seein' a hoop snake come a-rollin' out of the forest and just start whackin' at a young calf with the spike on its tail. I ain't never seen one but they say they's got like a horn spike on the end of their tail and they kill a thing by rollin' at it and hittin' it with that spike. And they roll, too, like in a circle. That's why they call 'em hoop snakes. Mean things, too. My grandma said it just plumb killed that calf, rollin' and spikin' it. Grandma told me she'd seen a hoop snake, or maybe someone told her, that just whacked its spike into a small tree and darn if that tree weren't dead in two days."

Jebber was horrified. "Jewel, if I ever seen a hoop snake rollin', I'd...I'd kill it! I tell you that. That's a bad thing that don't deserve to live. No siree."

"Grandma said they ain't around no more." She began to clean the table. "Now you get ready and go over to my brother's house. It's gonna be a big day."

Jebber nodded. "A big day."

Jewel smiled at her man. "And I feel that it's gonna be a right good day, too."

FOUR

At the Dillard house, the little family was eating Cassy's buttermilk biscuits, using them to sop up the bright golden egg yolks from Cassy's chickens, and devouring the sweet, crisp bacon. They were all hungry that morning, except for Boone. He let his eggs grow cold and just sipped at his coffee.

"Boone, what's wrong?" Cassy asked. "Didn't I make the eggs right?"

Boone didn't answer. He just stared off into the half-space where reality and imagination overlap. He seemed to be almost asleep.

Delilah barked at him. "Boone! Wake up and answer your wife. You ain't actin' right, boy."

And that seemed to do the trick. "Huh? What…what did you say?"

"I said wake up!"

Boone rubbed his eyes. "Oh… I must have drifted off. I was just… thinkin' about somethin'."

Cassy touched his hand. "What was you thinkin' about, honey?"

Boone looked into Cassy's eyes. "I… I don't remember now." And then he turned to Delilah. "It was a snake moon, Grandma."

"I know," Delilah said. "I tossed all night. And then I had bad dreams about Lem."

"I don't think I slept at all," Boone said.

"What you talkin' about, Pa?" Chap said. "You were sleepin' like a dead man. I couldn't wake you no how."

"Did you wake me up, Chap?"

18

"You know I did, Pa. You hugged me."

Boone stared off again and sipped at his coffee.

"Did you get the seeds in, Boone?" Cassy asked.

"No, Cassy. No, I didn't."

"But why not?"

"It just didn't seem right. There was somethin' in the air that...I don't know." And he went silent.

Cassy was baffled by her man's reluctance to be there for them. She had never seen him like this before, in such a haze, such a preoccupation.

"But it was the full moon in Taurus," Cassy said. "That's the time for plantin'. The best time. What could go wrong? It didn't rain or nothin'. It was a beautiful night."

Boone came out of the mist and looked deep into Cassy's eyes.

"It was a snake moon," he said.

And Cassy felt a brush of fear run across her back.

"You already said that, but I ain't ever heard of a snake moon. What is it?"

Delilah spoke up, taking command of the negative energy that was swirling around the breakfast table like a specter.

"Never you mind, daughter," Delilah said. "There's nothin' for you to be concerned about. And Boone, you eat them eggs now, you hear me? This is a special day and you can't be walkin' around in your dreamland. Chap's gonna kill a pig today!"

Chap was almost bursting with anticipation. "You bet I am, Grandma!"

"I know you are, boy," Delilah said. She banged her palms hard on the table, making the plates jump with a loud clatter, snapping Boone out of his trance and sending the bad energy back into its blackness. "Now come on, Boone. Eat up, and let's git that pig knife all sharpened for young Chap, here. And Cassy and Jewel and me got to git the fire goin' in the smokehouse, too."

Chap was up and out of his chair like a shot. "I'm gonna brush my teeth and go git Jebber right now!"

"You call out to Jebber and then knock on the door before you barge in there. You hear me?" Cassy said.

"But why, Ma?"

Cassy blushed. "Because they... uhh, might not be ready yet."

"So, I'll git 'em ready," Chap said.

"Chap, you just do like I tell ya and wait outside until they tell you to come in. Like a gentleman, you understand? Not like an animal."

"I ain't no animal, Ma."

Cassy smiled at her son. "Of course you ain't. Now come here and give me a hug, git yourself ready, and you men go kill that pig."

Chap almost knocked his mother off her chair in a bear hug rush, then squealed with delight and rushed off to get ready for his big day. Boone dipped his buttermilk biscuit into his golden egg yolk.

"Hey, these eggs is cold, Cassy!" he said.

Cassy and Delilah both had to laugh. Boone was back.

"Damn if I ain't hungry, too. And we got a big day today."

Boone was definitely back. Cassy was out of her chair and at the stove before anyone could blink, cracking four eggs into her black cast-iron frying pan that had been in the Dillard family for over thirty years now. It was seasoned with age and received the eggs lovingly, for that was its purpose in life and it was well up to the task.

"I'll fry you some fresh ones, Boone, and I'll warm that bacon for you, too," Cassy said, happy to feel her man's good and positive energy once again. "This is the last of the bacon, you know."

"I know that, darlin'," Boone said. "And that's why we're goin' out to git one of those yearling pigs that been workin' the mast in the forest. They's sweet now. Just like you, Cassy."

Cassy blushed, thinking of Jewel and Jebber that morning. She turned from her skillet to look at her man. "I love you, Boone," she softly said.

Boone looked at his wife with love in his eyes. "I love you too, Cassy. You know that."

"I know Boone."

Delilah couldn't take anymore. "I'm goin' to see about the fire in the smokehouse. You love birds don't need an old lady hangin' around whilst you get all mushy and into some kind of spring rut." And she was up and out the door, with Boone laughing his deep and wonderful chortle.

Out by the old smokehouse, Boone had built himself a

pottery kiln. He had attached it to the smokehouse built by his grandfather Lem, and he had designed it so that the fire in the center compartment could be used to heat either the kiln or the smokehouse by closing off one side or the other. When they used the smokehouse they didn't need nearly the wood they needed to heat the kiln, so Delilah could handle the task herself. But when it was time for Boone to fire his pottery, he had to be there. And Boone's pottery was unexpectedly beautiful for an untutored, backwoods farmer. He had the gift in his hands and he could fashion plates and cups and bowls and crocks and pitchers of the most pleasing shapes with the most luminous glazes. His work had a fineness and warmth to it that one simply did not see in the hills and hollows of backcountry Tennessee. His pieces had a glow that seemed to capture a bit of the sun itself. His plates radiated a warmth that felt like the warmth of the earth on a fine summer's day, and his cups and mugs seemed to actually keep coffee hot longer than they should have.

His graceful pitchers, his bowls and his crocks and jugs were always decorated with a bit of whimsy or a natural pattern that echoed the abundant life that surrounded them on all sides. Sometimes a few blades of grass, or a leaf, or a cloud, or just a graceful dripping of color from around the rim. Lately Boone had begun to use a more freeform approach to his glazing and the outcome always surprised him. It was as if he weren't in charge of the creation. He would dip the bowls in various glazing mixtures, apply random daubs, and place them in the kiln. Then the fire would work its alchemy and determine the ultimate outcome. The final colors and patterns came from the fire itself, and Boone loved the surprise of removing the finished pieces from the kiln. It was always a delight to him to see what the two of them together had created. Himself and the fire.

Consequently, Boone had supplied everything the two households needed for daily living and still had a small shed brim full of more pottery than the two families could use in a lifetime. For he just loved the creation and experimentation, and practiced it whenever he could. It was his hobby, and even more, his art.

FIVE

Chap came rushing out of the house calling to Jebber.

"Jebber! Hey, Jebber...git up!"

Delilah, looking through the farm's cords of oak and hickory for just the right blend of hard and sweet wood for the smokehouse, called back to Chap, "You be quiet, boy. Don't be runnin' and screamin' like a banshee. You's like to wake the dead with all that noise."

And Chap shouted back to his great-grandmother, "Yes, ma'am! I'll be quiet. *Hey, Jebber!*"

The door of Jewel and Jebber's cabin opened and out stepped the big, handsome child in the man's body. With an axe over his shoulder, no less.

"I'm here, Chap. And I'm ready to kill a pig!"

Chap shouted even louder, "Yippee, Jebber! So am I." And he raced up to Jebber and gave him a bear cub hug of love. Jebber patted his little nephew on the head and smiled at the ferocity of that hug.

"I love you, too, Chap."

Chap stood back a step. "How'd you know I was goin' to say that?"

"Well, you was, wasn't you?"

"Yeah, but how'd you know?"

"I could feel it in your arms, Chap. They said 'I love you' and I just said it back. And we's gonna kill us a *pig!* Is you ready?"

"I sure am, Jebber! I'm ready to do some killin'."

"*Hoo-whee!*" Jebber cried out. "Let's go git your pa."

"And let's git that pig knife!" Chap shrieked. "I want to hold that knife."

"Oh, you will, Chap. You'll be doin' the cuttin'. And yer pa and I made that knife sharp like a razor so you kin cut that pig like you was cuttin' butter!" And Jebber had to cry out again, "*Hoo-whee!*"

And Chap answered him back with his own high-pitched cry of excitement, "*Hoo-whee!*"

Jewel came out to join the two over-excited pig killers. "What you boys howlin' about?"

"I'm gonna kill a pig," Chap said.

Jewel smiled at her almost hysterical nephew. "I know you are, Chap. And if there was anyone around for fifty miles, they'd know it, too."

Jebber looked at his wife. "But there ain't nobody around, Jewel."

"I know there ain't, Jebber. I was just makin' a joke."

"I ain't never seen nobody around. This hollow is ours, it don't belong to nobody else."

"I know, Jebber."

"And if anybody came to take it away, I'd kill 'em!"

"I'd kill 'em too, Jewel," Chap piped in. "I'd git me that pig knife and kill anybody tried to take our farm away."

Jewel had to laugh. "You boys sure got killin' on your minds. Why don't you just find us a nice fat pig and kill that. 'Cause we's about run out of bacon and we ain't got no hams left at all."

"That's what we's gonna do!" Jebber said.

"And I get to kill it, Jewel!" Chap shouted.

Jewel smiled again. "Well, you two just go and get my brother and go get started with your killin'. We's gonna have us some fresh pork roast tonight and I can hardly wait. Now git!"

And the two boys—the man-boy and the little boy—raced off, howling like banshees, filled to overflowing with the joy of life and the coming of spring to Coker Creek Hollow.

And then Boone stepped out onto his front porch, holding the long, razor-sharp pig knife. He saw the two wildly running toward him. "Come on, boys. Let's go kill us a pig!"

And Chap and Jebber howled again. They had entered a state beyond excitement. A state of being that belonged to a more primitive time. A time when there was little difference between man and animal. They had entered a state in which only basic needs existed. Hunger, procreation, warmth, thirst.

Their frenzy had driven them slightly mad and they had receded into primordial beings. Back beyond the Indians. Back beyond anything any man could acknowledge in the Christian year of our Lord of 1863. They had entered into a blood lust.

"Let me have that knife, Pa!"

Boone carefully handed the honed blade to his son. It was almost a rite of passage, a handing of the sacred object from one generation to the next. "You be careful with this, son. It's sharp as a razor and it's like to cut your leg off if you ain't careful. You hear me?"

"I hear you, Pa," Chap said as he reverently held his hands out to receive the new steel of his manhood, passed to him by the leader of the tribe. "I'll be careful."

"I know you will, son." Boone patted his boy on the head in a sweet gesture of blessing, and time paused for an instant. An instant that had repeated itself for thousands of generations. This was what it was like to be father and son.

"Come on, you two!" Jebber shouted. "Let's get goin'."

"All right, Jebber," Boone said. "Let's do it. Let's go find us a big, fat, sweet pig!"

"*Hoo-whee!*" Jebber exclaimed.

"And *kill* it!" Chap shouted.

And the two boys raced off toward the woods with Boone trotting slowly behind them. Off toward the green wall and the wildness.

The two wives stood on their front porches and Delilah watched at the woodpile as their three men moved off into the unknown. They all waved and cried out, "Good luck!"

Then Boone stopped. He ran back to his wife, took her in his arms, and kissed her full on the mouth. "I love you, Cassy," he said. "Don't you never forget that."

Cassy's breath was taken away by the passion of that kiss, and she couldn't speak. She could only nod her head in understanding, gasping for air.

Then Boone ran to the woodpile, to Delilah. "I didn't get the seeds in, Nana. It wasn't right last night. Could you and Cassy and Jewel do it? The seeds and the golden water are just sittin' in the middle of the field, right where I left 'em."

Delilah nodded. "I knew sumpin' was wrong last night. Good thing you didn't put those seeds in. Wouldn't 'a come up right, anyway. 'A course we'll do it."

Boone hugged his grandmother. "I love you, too, Grandma. And I love this farm of ours."

The warmth of Boone's arms around her made Delilah smile. "I do, too, son," she said as she rested in his arms. Then she became the wise old owl again. "Now git and take care of those boys." She slapped him on the rump and cackled her laugh of a thousand years.

Boone ran over to Jewel and gave her a brotherly peck on the cheek. "It's gonna be a good day, Jewel."

Jewel smiled at her brother. "I believe it is, Boone. I do believe it is."

And then he raced off. To the west. Into the wilds. And the three women watched him disappear through the wall of new sprung green. And then the sun came up from behind the hills to the east, illuminating everything from a bright, cloudless sky. The sun's light was warm and good and the three women stood for a moment, feeling it on their faces. Letting its energy wash over them and warm their hearts, making them feel at peace with the world. And all three of them realized how good it was to be alive, and how blessed they were to all be living together on their homestead in Coker Creek Hollow. The earth had come to life again, and it was almost paradise.

SIX

In the midst of the deep forest, Boone had completely lost sight of Jebber and Chap. It was if they had been swallowed by the green. They were gone. Boone cried out to them in alarm. "Chap! Jebber! Where the hell are you two?"

But there was nothing. There was only the rustle of the leaves in the soft morning breeze. Even the birds had gone strangely silent. And Boone thought of last night's snake moon and the apparition. For he was now deep into where that apparition had emanated from, if there was anything there at all. But if there was, Boone was now where *it* was.

But he had no truck with superstitions of that sort. He didn't believe in spirits and ghosts. He knew the dead were dead. The living had nothing to fear from the dead. The living had, however, much to fear from the living. Boone knew this. But he also knew something happened to him last night, under the snake moon, and he shuddered at the thought.

And then heard it! Off in the distance. A screaming and caterwauling. Like banshees!

And he knew it was the boys. He ran toward the sound, through the dense vegetation, through the lush, fresh leaves of spring, through the soft new green that was everywhere around him, and the banshee howls grew louder. As he got closer he could almost distinguish three separate screams. Two seemed to be of an insane delight but the other was of pure terror.

He burst through the woods into a small clearing and there they were. Jebber was riding the back of a bucking hog, bent over it holding its tail and one of its ears and screaming, *"Hoo-whee! Piggy! Piggy! Piggy!"*

Chap was running around and around in circles, waving the killing knife and screaming his lungs out. The pig was in mortal fear and screaming its lungs out, too.

Boone stopped and had to laugh to himself at how ridiculous his boys were. The two wildmen had found their quarry, but now, unfortunately, were trying to torment it to death.

"You two stop that now!" Boone shouted.

"Pa," squealed Chap. "We got him! We got him."

"I got him good, Boone!" Jebber shouted. "We was waitin' on you before Chap killed him."

"Can I kill him now, Pa?"

"Hold your horses, boy," Boone said to his son. "And Jebber, get off the pig. Don't be doin' him like that. You 'bout to worry that poor creature to death."

Jebber climbed off the pig, holding it tightly around the neck and hanging on to its tail. "Yes, Boone," he contritely said.

"We share the earth with these creatures, Jebber," Boone said. "We have to take care of them. We have to be good to them. They feed us and we have to thank them for that. They give us their lives so's we can live. That's a fine thing they do and we can't be scarin' the bejesus out of them. You hear me... both of you?"

Jebber and Chap grew silent with shame. "Yes, Pa. Yes, Boone," they said almost in unison.

"This here pig's spirit is goin' back into the energy," Boone continued. "And that's the same energy we all go back to. It's the same energy we all come from, too. We come from the energy, we live our lives, and we go back into the energy when we die. It's the same for that pig as it is for all of us. And it's the same for everything that lives on this here earth. All the birds and plants and fishes and...everything. We are all of us the energy. And that energy is the light, and that light is the light of God. You understand me?"

And of course the two wild men didn't understand a word of what Boone was saying. They only had one thing on their minds. And that was killing.

"I just want you two to always remember what I just said. You hear me?"

"Yes, Pa. Yes, Boone," the killing twins humbly said.

"Now! Chap, is you ready to kill that pig?" Boone shouted, changing the mood back to harsh reality.

Chap squealed, "I's ready, Pa!"

"Well, Jebber," Boone said. "You hold that there pig's head way back so's Chap can get a nice clean cut at his neck."

"I got 'em, Boone." And Jebber sat on the screaming hog, grabbed both ears, and pulled them back until the pig's snout pointed straight up into the high blue sky.

"Now, Chap, you go cut that pig's throat just like Jebber and me showed you before."

Chap's eyes took on a maniacal glint and he became strangely silent. He held the razor-sharp blade up high at his shoulder and moved forward on his first step into manhood.

"Cut him clean, Chap," Jebber said. "From ear to ear."

And as Chap was about to strike, Boone said, "Don't cut him till you thank him for bein' alive, Chap."

Chap stopped the blade short of the pig's gullet, put the knife back at shoulder height, its tip pointing to the sky, and softly said, "Thank you, Mister Pig." Then, with a furious stroke, slashed the blade down out of the heavens and across the pig's throat, cutting it in one great swipe from ear to ear. Clean and quick. And the pig did not utter a sound. It was as if Chap's thanking him had appeased the soul of the beast and had put him at ease. The pig's eyes grew wide with death as his life's blood flew everywhere. Covering Chap and the killing blade with warm, red liquid. Smearing everything. Running down Chap's face and arms. Rivulets of blood. A torrent of blood. Smearing and coating everything with the sweet smell of death.

And Jebber howled like a madman into the heavens. "Hoo-whee! *Heeyah!* You did it, Chap! You killed him clean. *Hoo-whee!*"

But Chap was frozen with the knowledge of what he had done. He had killed so that his family could live. And he began to shake, with the blood dripping off his face and off his hands. He could no longer control his body and his limbs began to twitch convulsively and the blood dripped off him, onto the ground, and began to puddle at his feet.

And then the pig gave a death rattle and fell on its side. Its life gone. And the energy left it and rejoined the energy of all creation.

Chap cried out as the pig fell to the earth and Boone rushed forward to grab his little boy in a protective hug. He lifted Chap up off his feet as the killing blade slipped from Chap's hand, wet with blood, and fell to the forest floor by the side of its victim. Boone pressed Chap against his chest and turned away from the slaughter as the boy began to sob, deep within himself. The sobs of a childhood now lost forever.

"Don't you cry, son," Boone said softly. "You done well. The pig's gone to God now."

And Chap wept, uncontrollably.

"You took one life to save many lives, Chap. To save your family." And Boone hugged his boy close to him, close to the energy of his heart so that his son could feel the love he had for him.

"You did fine, Chap!" Jebber shouted. "We's got us ham and bacon, now! Hoo-whee!"

And Chap regained himself as his two heroes praised him. And his crying stopped and he became proud of his feat.

"I did it, didn't I, Pa?"

And Boone felt his own pride at seeing his son take his first step into inevitable manhood.

"Yes, you did, son. Now you go run off into the forest and wipe that blood off with some leaves," Boone said as he lowered Chap to the ground. "You don't need to see what Jebber and me's gonna do now. You go clean up."

"Yes, Pa," Chap said as he dashed across the little clearing and into the green forest.

"And look for that white turkey," Boone called to him. "You never know, he might just be out there waitin' for you. He's good luck, ya know!"

And Chap was gone

"I ain't seen that white turkey yet, Boone," Jebber said. "I sure want to see him and get some good luck."

Boone laughed. "Why Jebber, your life ain't nothin' but good luck."

"You ever seen him, Boone? 'Cause your life's good luck, too."

Then Boone grew silent and he looked off into the depths of the wilderness.

"I might have seen him last night," he finally said. "And if I did, he ain't good luck."

Then the two men set to stringing up the pig by its hind legs over a stout, low-hanging tree limb. They did this by scraping the hide from the hamstring and exposing it on both legs, then a strong stick about two and a half feet long was slipped behind the exposed tendons. They slipped the pig over the cleared tree limb, through his legs, suspending him upside down with all his dead weight resting on the stick. Then Jebber worked the knife across Chap's killing cut, opening the flesh all the way back to the neck bone, and the pig drained clean of all its blood.

Boone and Jebber could only stand there in silence as they watched the blood slowly fall into a puddle beneath the upside-down pig. And the only sound was of the breeze blowing through the new green leaves, and the buzz of the blue flies that came to the smell of death.

SEVEN

"There's a thing! There's a thing comin'!" Chap screamed from just inside the green wall as he burst into the little clearing, running for all he was worth, as if he were fleeing a ghost.

Boone and Jebber were shaken out of their trance. "What is it, son?" cried Boone.

"It's a thing!" Chap screamed, still wet with blood, as he raced into the safety of his father's arms. "I ain't never seen nothin' like it."

Jebber felt an icelike grip of fear attach itself to his spine. "Wha', what's it like, Chap?" he stuttered.

Chap clung to Boone, face buried in his father's belly, afraid to look back. "It's got two legs upfront and two...uhh, like wheels behind! And it's big! Bigger than a man. And it's makin' an awful bangin' noise, like it's all iron or somethin'."

Even Boone grew afraid at the picture Chap painted. We gotta get outta here!" Chap continued. "It's comin' this way. It's comin' after us!"

And Boone, normally a man of courage and not given to childish fears or flights of fancy, thought of the snake moon last night. And the apparition.

"Let's get that pig down, Jebber. I don't want to see that thing. Let's get home!"

And Jebber swung his axe at the pig's legs just below the support stick. One swing cut through both legs and the pig fell onto the forest floor in a heap. Jebber handed Boone the axe and hoisted the pig onto his broad shoulders, and as he did so, the weight of the pig caused a final gush of blood to flow out of it, covering Jebber in a sickly red. He bounced it into balance on his shoulders and even more blood spilled out. He looked at the little boy. "Come on, Chap," he said. "Let's git home!"

And the two boys, the man-boy and the little, frightened boy, moved off, away from the thing. Boone turned for one last look and thought he heard, deep in the woods, the sound of clattering, like metal, with the sound of a moan, all anguished and terrible, mixed into it. And he ran off.

Back at the Dillard homestead the women had the huge iron pot of scalding water ready to receive the pig and soften its bristles. And the fire was also going in the smokehouse with a nice blend of hickory and oak that Delilah had prepared as she had done for the last fifty years. With just enough oak for heat and just enough hickory for sweetness. And a sack of salt was at hand to rub down the hams and shoulders before they went into the smokehouse.

The women were in the field planting the corn seeds and sprinkling a little of the vortex-created golden water over them, as Boone was supposed to have done the night before. They worked at a pace that bespoke contentment and happiness. They moved easily in the field, working in three parallel rows, talking softly to each other.

"Why didn't Boone do this last night, Grandma?" Cassy asked.

"I don't know, child," Delilah said. "All's I know is that it were a snake moon last night."

That caught Jewel's attention. "What'cha mean by a snake moon, Grandma?"

Delilah stopped and stood up from her bent over, planting stance. She stretched her arms over her head, reaching up to the sun, stretching out her compacted body.

"Oh, that sun feels good. I can't stay bent over too long like I used to when I was your age. A couple of minutes and I got to reach up to Mister Sun and say howdy to him." She twisted slowly to one side and then the other, with her arms up to the heavens, almost in worship of the sky. "And I want you girls to git in the habit of saying howdy to the sun, too. You should thank him for comin' up each day and goin' across the land to warm it and callin' everything to life like he does. 'Cause without him there ain't nothin'. He's the pure energy. Or as close as we get to the pure energy, 'cause that's God. And if you hold your hands up and feel the heat of the light from the sun, why, you'll feel God!"

And the old woman broke into a smile and stretched her arms out as far as she could, up into the sky.

"Come on, you girls try it. Just feel that light with your hands."

And the two young women stood up from their planting and raised their hands to the sun.

"Now close yer eyes and feel the sun on yer face and in the palms of yer hands. Kinda round yer hands like you was cuppin' a sun beam and just hold 'em out to Mister Sun."

The girls stretched themselves out, heads tilted back, faces to the sun, hands cupped to catch the light.

"Now, don't that feel good?" Delilah said.

And the three women stood in the middle of their field in Coker Creek Hollow, arms raised to the sky in the freshness of spring, with a soft breeze blowing in the air and the sun warming everything beneath its merciful glow.

And after a moment Cassy cried out, "I can feel it, Grandma! I can feel the energy! It's in my hands."

"Yes it is, girl," Delilah said. "Now feel it in yer heart. Let it warm yer soul."

And Cassy held her hands out to the light and started to sway ever so slightly as if she were entering into a rapture. "Oh, Grandma," she said, "it feels so good. I got the energy right here in my heart." And she brought her hands down out of the sky and placed them, one over the other, on her chest. "It's inside of me! It's the energy of the sun. But…but, it's the energy of everything!"

And she raised her arms to the sky again and began to sway. "My God, Grandma," she cried out. "It's all energy! We're *all* energy. Everything is. And it's all God!" And tears of joy began to well up in her eyes. "Grandma, it's so beautiful to be alive. I never knew just how beautiful it really is!" And she rocked and swayed in the light, her arms stretched out to Heaven.

Then Delilah took Cassy in her arms and hugged her. "That's it, darlin'," she said. "That's it. You're in the light, now!"

"I *am* the light, Grandma!" And the tears of joy came flowing out of Cassy's eyes. And Delilah just hugged her, laughing and beginning to cry herself. And Cassy laughed and cried and hugged Delilah in return as Jewel came over and embraced the two of them.

And there they stood, the three women, locked in an embrace of love, crying and laughing and being alive in the light of the sun in the sky. Crying and laughing in the planting field of Coker Creek Hollow. And it was almost paradise.

And then the men burst through the green wall. Covered in blood, carrying the pig and their killing tools.

"There's a thing! There's a thing comin'!" screamed Chap.

EIGHT

"Get back to the houses," Boone shouted to the women; and the moment of peace in the spring planting field was over. Cassy, Jewel, and Delilah broke from their heavenly embrace as reality intruded upon them.

"What is it, Boone?" Cassy shouted back.

He came up to her breathing hard and with a look in his eyes that made Cassy afraid. "I don't know," he said. "I ain't seen it, but I heard it."

Jebber was right behind him, easily bearing the weight of the hog. "Jewel," he said, "we got to run! It's big and mean, and it's got legs and wheels, and…and it's comin' to…to eat us!"

Chap screamed again, "That's right! It's comin' to eat us!"

They fell back to their compound. Cassy rushed into the house and gathered the baby up out of his crib. Jebber moved quickly to the smokehouse where the women had prepared a cauldron of steaming water, lifted the pig up off his shoulders and dumped it on the ground next to the cauldron. Then he picked up a long sling blade and joined Boone with the axe at the ready and Chap with the pig knife at his shoulder. The three men formed a wall of protection in front of the women as Cassy rejoined them with the baby held tightly against her breast.

They stood frozen in the ice of unknowing, staring into the green forest for a sign of anything, any movement. And then they heard it! A clattering and a clanking and the moaning that Boone thought he had heard in the forest. But now he knew it was real. And the fear gripped all of their spines, causing them to grow cold inside, as the sun seemed to withdraw its heat from everything. Even the baby could sense the approaching darkness and it began to wail with high, piercing shrieks. The women huddled closer to their men as the clanking and banging grew louder. The men squeezed their weapons even tighter, hardening their hands for the coming battle with the unknown thing.

Then, from out of the green wall, trundled a gnarled gnome of a man. Bent at the waist, covered with a blanket, his wrists wrapped by rope wound round the stubby wagon shafts of a two-wheeled cart that was piled high with boxes of sundries, pots and pans and knives and shovels and tools of all description hanging off the boxes, clattering together like the cymbals of Xerxes. He had strapped himself into the harness, the better to pull his rickety rig, and he bucked and struggled and moaned with each tug as the wheels hung themselves up on rocks and roots strewn across the forest floor.

When "the thing" broke free of the forest and entered the field, the gnome raised himself up from his crouch, the blanket falling from his shoulders, and looked up into the heavens.

"Thank you, Lord, for a bit of smoothness," he said in a cracked and parched voice. And then, as his eyes came down out of the sky, he saw his adversaries, huddled together in a defensive line with steel weapons raised and ready for blood.

"My friends," he called out. "The Lord has truly blessed you this day. I've come into your lives to bring you all the things you need." And he began to pull again, clattering his rig across the newly planted field.

Boone lowered his axe to the ground and laughed to himself. "So that's the monster in the forest, is it? That old peddler-man?"

"I reckon it ain't no monster at all," Jebber said. And Boone slapped him on the back and laughed out loud, shaking the ice off his spine. And then the others laughed, shattering the darkness of their fear and allowing the sun to regain its warmth.

Cassy and Jewel both giggled girlishly as Delilah smiled at their silliness. "Pshaw, Chap," she said. "That thing ain't gonna eat us. It's gonna try and *sell* us somethin'."

"Hell," Jebber said, "maybe we could eat *it*! Boone, do you think it got some candy in there? I shore would like some candy."

And everyone laughed at the big man-boy.

"I'd like some candy, too, Pa," Chap said hungrily.

"Well, boys, it looks like he's got just about everything in there,"

Boone said. "And ain't none of it that we need."

" 'Cept candy," Jebber replied.

And as the old peddler-gnome clanked forward, he saw and understood the very lushness and ripeness of the Dillard homestead in Coker Creek Hollow and he spoke out into the air, "And God said, *Let the earth bring forth grass, the herb yielding seed, and the fruit tree yielding fruit after his kind, whose seed is in itself, upon the earth: and it was so.*"

Boone came forward out of the defensive line, the axe resting lightly on his shoulder. The peddler-gnome dropped to his knees, head bowed, and continued his paean: "*And the earth brought forth grass and grain and herb yielding seed after his kind, and the tree brought forth fruit, whose seed was in itself: and God saw it was good.*"

He lifted his face that seemed to beam in exaltation, and then the light went out of his eyes as he saw Boone standing over him, taking the axe off his shoulder and wrapping both hands around its shaft. Then he saw Jebber rush up with the sling blade in his hand. And he was afraid. He shook his head and looked to Heaven.

"Ain't that just like you. Give a man a peek at paradise, then dash him all to hell."

Harnessed in his cart and down on his knees like some bound penitent, the peddler looked at Boone and Jebber with resignation.

"Boys, I am bone weary and my belly's as empty as my pockets. The choice is yours. Kill me, or feed me."

And then Boone swung the axe in a high arc over his head, seemingly to cut off the peddler's head.

"Damn you!" the peddler shouted at either Boone, or God, or both.

And the axe came flying down out of the sky, the sun glinting off the polished edge. The gnome shut tight his eyes as the axe flew past his head and cleanly cut the cord that wrapped his wrist and the wagon shaft, cutting one hand free. The axe swung again and the other hand was free. The gnome clasped them together in prayer.

"Thank you, Lord."

Jebber danced an idiot's jig behind Boone. "You got candy?"

Boone lifted the peddler off his knees. "Sure, we'll feed you," he said. "We take care of all of God's creatures here in the hollow." And then he laughed his deep belly-laugh, relieved that his fears had been unfounded foolishness. "And mister, you *almost* look like one yourself."

The peddler cackled a dry, raspy laugh. "Thank you for the compliment, son. And the name's Elijah Beasley."

"You got candy?" Jebber squealed.

"I got everything, boy. That cart there carries the world."

Boone laughed again. "And it looks like you been carryin' the world on your shoulders."

"My mule died," the gnome said. "And I had him for thirteen years. He was a good mule, too. He was my friend. And then he jest up and died about a week ago." He looked over at his cart. "Been pullin' the world ever since."

"You get Jebber a little candy, and some for my boy," Boone said. "Then we's gonna feed you till yer stuffed like a turkey for Thanksgiving. We got ourselves a fresh pig! And my boy killed it. His first one."

Jebber swung his sling blade over his head. "Cut it clean," he said. "Right across the neck. Ear to ear." And he howled again with the memory. *"Oww whee-haw!"*

Elijah looked at Boone. "He's an excitable one, ain't he?"

"He ain't all there," Boone replied.

"I can tell that. Well, then, let's git him some candy before he does me in with that there sling blade. Come on, boy!"

"His name's Jebber."

"Come on, Jebber! Let's find that candy the Lord has provided."

"Hoo-whee!" shouted Jebber. "Candy!"

"And if I can get you to haul my wagon over to the houses, there, I'll give you a piece of candy for free."

"Hoo-whee!" Jebber shouted again as Boone had to laugh at his drooling man-boy brother-in-law.

NINE

After they had boiled and skinned and dressed and smoked the pig and all its parts, the entire family sat down to dinner at Boone's table. Cassy had prepared a fresh pork-shoulder roast with vinegared dandelion greens, mashed potatoes, and butter and biscuits. They all sat at Boone's table, watching Elijah Beasley devour the last of his second plateful of Cassy's meal.

"This here's darn fine eatin', ma'am."

"Thank you, sir," said Cassy. "But I can't take credit for it. I learnt it from Delilah, here."

"Well, then I thank both of you. One for the makin' and one for the teachin'. And ain't that the way the Lord intended it to be, each generation comes to pass and leaves its mark on the generation what comes after it. And all things must pass, but the earth abideth."

"Them's fine words, Mr. Beasley," Boone said. "I do believe you're a man of God."

"No, son. I seen too much out there to actually believe in God anymore." And he cleaned his plate with the last chunk of biscuit, popped it into his mouth, and smiled. "Until, 'a course, I seen your place here and then it kinda renewed my faith."

"What you seen that I ain't seen?" Delilah asked. "And I ain't lost no faith in life."

"Beggin' your pardon, old woman, but I seen Hell."

"You ain't!" Jebber threw in.

"Yes, I have, Jebber. I seen the wasteland. I seen men torn to pieces, broken bodies covering fields with blood like a river. Horses and mules and men. I seen carnage, boy."

"Where you seen that?" Jebber asked, astonished.

And Elijah threw his hands out wide. "Everywhere! It's all around you people."

"You're makin' it up," Jebber said back. "It ain't around us."

"It's the war, you fool!"

"Ain't no war," said Boone.

And the peddler-gnome looked at all their faces and saw they had no fear in them. "What have you people done, turned a blind eye on the whole damn conflagration?" There was no answer from anyone. Elijah threw his head back and cackled to the heavens. "Oh, you're clever, ain't you?" And then he looked at the family. "By some meager mercy of God, it ain't yet tore through your woods, has it."

Chap jumped in. "Mister, what war are you talkin' of?"

"I don't know that's it's my place to tell you," and his eyes met the wisdom of Delilah's. "But of course…I must."

Then he pulled a pouch from his overalls, pushed back from the table, stretched his legs, and tamped tobacco into his pipe. He lit up and took a long draw from his pipe and a cloud of white smoke encircled his head like the mist that had encircled Boone the night before.

"It began like some grand carnival. 'Twas April, two years past. In the dead of night, Rebel guns boomed upon Fort Sumter in Charleston Harbor. The blazing shot streaked the sky like fireworks on the Fourth of July, and townsfolk lined the rooftops and waterfront to enjoy the jubilee. But when flame and smoke plumed over the Federal bastion, the sound of weeping women was heard. You could hear it coming up from underneath all the cheers and shouts. In my mind, it weren't the cannon-shot, but those cries, that signaled the slaughter to come."

Boone had brought one of his fine yellow-ware jugs to the table. It held his home-brewed corn liquor and he poured Elijah a hefty draught.

"Thank you, my friend," Elijah said as he knocked back a copious slug of the white lightning. "Ain't had a taste of corn in quite a while now."

"Go on with your story, sir," Cassy said.

"Well, ma'am…it seemed the armies massed for the first big battle in a place called Bull Run. When the haze of dust and smoke and burnt powder blew clear, near to four thousand men lay dead or maimed upon that fallow field."

"Hold yer yarn a bit, Mr. Beasley," Boone said. "Just who's fightin' who?"

"Most every man in the nation, son. 'Cept for those of us here at this table. The South split from the North. It's state against state, brother fightin' brother, kin killin' kin." And he took another sip of his corn liquor.

"As time wore by, nothin's changed save the numbers. The affray at Shiloh left ten thousand killed and crippled on either side. A week of warrin' in the Shenandoah Valley, and forty thousand fell. A single day's scrap along Antietam Creek bloodied twenty thousand more. There was a stretch of road there, sunken by the weight of wagons, and Johnny Reb lined it for half a mile like a dug-in rifle trench. Wave upon wave, the Northern brigades swarmed that long battlement. Regimental chaplains rode back and forth, screaming absolution as the troops ran past, headlong to certain death. God's ears must've heard the pleas of those newly blessed boys in blue, for somehow they broke the Rebel line. Bodies lay four and five abreast for half a mile long. And now when they speak of that carriageway, they call it Bloody Lane."

And then there was silence at the table. They were all struck dumb by the horror of the peddler-gnome's story. And it seemed as if the flutter of the wings of the angel of death could be heard above their heads, deep in the core of their mute agony.

Then Cassy broke the spell of that dark apparition. "But what is it they's fightin' over?"

Elijah sucked at his pipe, blew a white shroud over the table, sipped as his corn liquor, and quietly said, "The coloreds."

It hung in the air for an instant, like a hummingbird, and then it plunged into their understanding.

"The coloreds?" Boone said with great disbelief.

"Yep. The coloreds," the gnome replied.

Jebber just couldn't help himself. He began to giggle. And his high-pitched imitation of a mule's heehaw infected the table and made Jewel and Cassy and Chap all fall in step with his laughter.

Even Boone had to laugh. "But that don't make no sense," he said. "What did the coloreds do?" Did they all do somethin' bad that they's fightin' over them?"

"Well...I reckon so," the gnome said. "It seems they was born a different color from white folks."

Cassy spoke up after getting control of her giggles. "Of course they is, that's why they's the coloreds. If they wasn't a different color, we'd all be white!" And she started laughing again at the obviousness of her statement. And that only added fuel to Jebber's heehawing which in turn stoked Chap's giggles and refired Jewel's laughter. They were having a fine old time at the peddler's expense.

"Ain't nothin' wrong with being a different color," Boone said over the ruckus. "They must've done somethin' bad to make the states fight over them."

The gnome poured himself another cupful of corn liquor from Boone's jug. It was a particularly fine jug with a blue glazed edging around the lip and the barest outline of a few elm leaves spraying out from their stem against the lustrous yellow of the jug's round body.

The gnome rubbed his hands over the surface of the jug after he poured his drink, seeing its beauty for the first time. "This is a right fine jug," he said.

The peddler sipped his liquor. "This cup is right fine, too. Almost delicate in the hand."

Boone smiled. "I like to make things nice. Ain't no reason for bad work. Bad work's just lazy work."

"Well, this jug and cup sure ain't lazy work," the peddler said. "You got more?"

"Everything you ate on is mine."

Jebber had finally gotten the mule in his throat under control. "Boone's got a whole shed fulla jugs and plates and cups an'...I don't know *what* all he's made."

"I like to see that there shed," the peddler said.

"First you get back to yer story," Boone said. "I want to know what the coloreds did that was so bad."

"Well, son, I reckon they just want to be free."

"Ain't they free now?" asked Cassy.

"No ma'am, they ain't. They's slaves."

"What's a slave?" asked Jebber.

The peddler-gnome snorted at Jebber's lack of knowledge. "Ya big galoot. A slave's a black man what's owned by a white man."

"How can one man own another man?" Chap asked.

"That's the way the country's organized, boy."

"But that ain't right," Cassy said. "The Lord don't allow one man to own another. The Hebrews was slaves in the Bible and that weren't right."

The peddler-gnome sipped his corn from Boone's delicate cup. *"And the Lord delivered the children of Israel from out of bondage so they could be free to testify to the glory of God."*

"Amen to that," Delilah said.

"And now we are at the time of the great deliverance of the coloreds from out of their bondage," the peddler said.

"Amen, again," Delilah said. And Boone and Cassy and Jewel joined her with "amens" of their own.

" 'Cept this time," the peddler said, "the whites are gonna kill each other over the coloreds. And Lord God in Heaven they are doin' a most magnificent job of killin' themselves. There is the stench of death upon the land." And the peddler-gnome began to weep from exhaustion, unable to control the emotions of what he had seen. "And I cannot get the smell of it from out of my nostrils." Then he cried out, "Oh, Lord!" as his head fell down onto the table. His shoulders shook with deep sobs and the assembled family watched in silence, knowing in their hearts that the horror that he spoke of must be true.

TEN

Cassy had provided a pallet for Elijah Beasley to stay the night, and come the next morning—after fitful sleep filled with terrible dreams of mutilation and horror—the family awoke to a bright and clean dawn. The light washed away the evil of their night terrors and they all seemed to be in a mood that matched the splendid morning. And yet something dark had been loosed in all of them.

Breakfast was greedily consumed and then Mr. Beasley invited all of them to examine his wares.

"I got things y'all ain't never seen before. C'mon, and let your desires have their freedom." Then he leered at the young women. "And I know a thing or two about desires." Cassy and Jewel blushed and turned their eyes from his penetrating gaze. "We all have them, and they're natural. They ain't nothin' to be ashamed of. They come with bein' human. Why, desire is the very bedrock of the human condition. And now it's time for all of you to yield to *your* desires. Come on!"

And they all dashed out to the sutler wagon, Chap and Jebber in the lead yelping for candy. Cassy and Jewel right behind them, and even old Delilah hurried along, intrigued with the possibilities of acquisition. Boone brought up the rear, smiling at his family's excitement that had seemingly cleansed their minds of the horror of the peddler-gnome's story from the night before.

Mr. Beasley grabbed Boone's arm. "Son, there ain't nothin' much there for you. Why don't you show me your handiwork? If it's as fine as what we ate on last night, I might just have a proposition for you." And his eyes gleamed with a strange light as he spoke.

The two men walked over to the storage shed that held Boone's stoneware as the family scrambled over the wagon like ants over a piece of rotted meat, unleashing their desires.

Boone opened the door of the shed and a golden light seemed to pour forth from the interior like the light from one of Pharaoh's shrines in ancient Egypt when the sun would penetrate deep into the tabernacle on the dawning of the day of the summer solstice, illuminating one of the golden statues that had been shrouded in darkness for the entire year. And the peddler-gnome was amazed. He stepped into the shed like a priest of Amon-Re stepping into the sanctuary of Isis. He took one of the jugs from a shelf and held it like some holy relic of a faith long since lost behind the veil of time. His hand curved over the body of the jug, feeling its pleasing shape. He held it up to the light, admiring its golden sheen and the delicate pattern of blades of grass inscribed on its surface. Then he took another and another from off the shelves: bowls and plates and pitchers and urns and gravy boats and platters. Admiring them all, touching them all.

"I been through many a holler," the gnome said. "And I know the Great Road pottery, and I know the redware from Sullivan County. I know the work of Abraham and Martin Cain, and I seen Jesse Hancher's jugs and such, and James Davis's work out of Washington County. But I ain't never seen work like this."

He stopped for a breath and wheezed into the musky air of the shed. Boone took him out into the light, the peddler-gnome still clutching a golden pitcher.

"Boy, you got a touch," the gnome said. "People should know your name. It should be etched upon your art."

"It is," Boone said.

The gnome turned the pitcher upside down and looked at the base. "Boone Dillard!" he shouted, reading the name on the bottom. "1862! Are they all dated?"

Boone smiled. "Dated and signed. They're mine and I'm proud of 'em."

"Right you should be, Boone Dillard. And you should be *famous* because of your art." The gnome's eyes gleamed. "And you should be *rich*, too." He touched Boone's arm and grinned. "You'd like that, wouldn't you?" Then, before Boone could answer, he started to wheeze again. He handed the pitcher to Boone, took a stained handkerchief from his back pocket and coughed a tubercular rasp into it. His body shook with the force of the cough, and then another came, and then three more in quick succession. And Boone knew that Mr. Beasley did not have long to live.

When the spasms had subsided, the peddler-gnome laid a congratulatory hand on Boone's arm and pulled him into his confidence. "Looky, here's what we'll do. You got a mule ain't you?"

"I got a mule," Boone answered.

"Fine. Then what say you lend me that mule? I'll hitch him up to my cart, pack on as much of your stoneware as I can carry, and I'll tote it, at no cost to you, all the way down to Chattanooga. And son, I'll sell your wares and fetch you more money than you ever dreamed of. Then I'll journey back to ya, return your mule and divvy up the proceeds. Hell, if you want, I'll even do it again!" And he laughed and squeezed Boone's arm. "What you say, son?"

Boone looked at the tempter, then at the pitcher in his hands. He had never realized that his work, the work that he loved doing, might just be valuable. He knew what he did was good, but the idea of its potential worth to other people, especially people in the big city, delighted him. It was a validation of his own worth as a man.

"Tell you what, Mr. Beasley," Boone said, his eyes growing narrow and calculating. "What say I borrow *your* cart. Hitch up my mule, tote my own wares, and sell 'em my ownself. An' if Jebber over there don't squash yer runty bones by accidentally steppin' on you one day while I'm gone, you just might get yer cart back. 'Course, you'll have to pay me for the food y'eat while I'm gone."

The gnome knew he had been bested. "You, sir, drive a hard bargain," he said, shaking his head in defeat.

"Heck, I didn't ask for you to be sent here. Yet you up and appeared outta the woods. An' already I'm fillin' yer belly with my food, givin' you drink, and a place to lay yer head."

"That was might gracious of you," the gnome said. "And I aim to remedy that debt right now."

He began to walk off toward the sutler's wagon. Boone watched him and saw that his family no longer swarmed its contents. They just stood there, looking at the wagon, emptily.

"Ain't nothin' here we need, Mr. Beasley," Cassy said as the gnome shuffled up to them.

The glint of seduction reappeared in Elijah Beasley's eyes. "But is there anything you *want*, ladies?"

"We want yer candy!" Chap shouted as he stuffed his pockets with gaudily wrapped sweets.

"I love candy," Jebber added through a mouthful of sticky taffy.

"It's all dross," Delilah said.

"You ain't got nothin' but broken clocks and pots with no handles and dirty linens and bad-cut dresses," Jewel said petulantly.

"I'll consider that candy payment for your food and lodging, Mr. Beasley," Boone said as he came up and put an arm around Cassy. "I think that'll be fair."

"Done, sir," the gnome said. "Then it seems I have no other temptations to offer you people." He looked at his sutler's wagon and gave out a deep sigh. "As the Lord giveth, so also does he taketh away. *And He sent them out of the Garden to dwell in the land of Nod, somewhere east of Eden.*"

Elijah Beasley scurried over to his load of trappings, securing them, then stepped between the wagon shafts like an overburdened beast. He strapped himself to the left shaft and called to Chap. "Help me here, boy." And Chap secured the gnome's forearm to the other shaft. And then the gnome called to Jebber, "Give me a push to get me started, you big ox." Jebber complied, and with his shoulder to the load and a feral grunt, he began to propel the entire cart forward toward the green forest, heading south. The gnome rose up into the air from the force of Jebber's push. "Whee! Now that's the push I need all the way to Atlanta." The wagon shafts settled back down and the peddler-gnome was off and running, off into the green, off to his next temptation.

The Dillards and the Stubbs watched the cart disappear into the wilderness, clanking and rattling all the way. Boone laughed. "An' I thought that old fool was a monster!"

They all laughed, except Delilah. "Maybe he is," she said from her knowledge beyond their years. "Maybe he just is."

And a silence descended on the families. A silence that held their breaths for a heartbeat and the space between their heartbeats. Then it unleashed them, and they could breathe again.

"Let's get started, Jebber!" Boone said with great animation. "We's got work to do." And he strode off toward his pottery shed.

"What we got to do?" Jebber asked.

Boone looked back over his shoulder, not breaking stride. "We're goin' to the big city!"

ELEVEN

Boone and Jebber wrapped each piece of pottery with straw and built up a small hillock of objects. Boone made sure to include a variety of only his best work for he had taken the bait of the peddler-gnome and was determined to sell his creations in the big city. And for a fine profit, too.

"I bet that old Mr. Beasley seen a good bit of this world, don't you, Jebber?" Boone asked.

"I don't rightly know what all he seen," Jebber said.

Boone spoke more to the air, and to himself, than to Jebber. "And I reckon he knows what he's talkin' about, 'cause he's seen it all." He took a small box from a shelf. It was delicate, with a small bird's head at the top of the lid, perfect to hold a fine lady's talcum powder. "This should bring a nice price, if we can find the right buyer." Boone held the box gently in his hand and wrapped it carefully. "Don't you think so, Jebber?"

Jebber merely grunted, not knowing anything about delicacy.

"Wouldn't that be somethin'?" Boone went on dreamily. "To see all he seen with yer own two eyes. Wouldn't that, Jebber?"

"Not if we have to see any dead bodies," Jebber said. "An' I don't want to see any dead horses, Boone. I love horses. I wish we had one so's we could ride it."

"We'll get one when I sell my wares, Jebber. I promise you that. A nice horse, just for you."

"Can I name it, Boone?"

"Of course you can. It'll be yours, won't it?"

"I'm gonna name him Lightnin' Rod!" Jebber said proudly.

"That's a fine name," Boone said.

"But I don't want to see no dead bodies like that Mr. Beasley seen."

"We ain't goin' nowhere near no war," Boone said. "We's just goin' to the big city, where all the rich people live. An' we's gonna see things we ain't never seen before. Like, you remember that time we ventured on down to Turtle Town to swap pelts for pig iron so's we could forge our blades?"

"I sure do, Boone. That ol' mule shrunk half a foot draggin' back that load."

Boone laughed at his man-boy brother-in-law. "Yep, I think she did. Anyhow, man there said his iron was bein' bought to lay rails for some train that could travel in a day further than you could ride Lightnin' Rod in a week. I didn't buy him at his word. But now, for some reason, I believe I do. I'd like to see that train. I'd like to take me a ride upon it."

Jebber was moving the hillock of wrapped pottery onto the family cart that was used for hauling hay at the end of the season. He had worked up a good sweat in the heat of the noonday sun. "You reckon they got ice?" he said, mopping his brow.

Boone was called back, out of his daydream. "Ice?"

"Yesiree," Jebber said. "Ice. Right now, in this heat. And in the summertime, too. Heck, what good is ice when it comes in winter? I sure could do with a piece of ice. You reckon there's some place that's got ice when it's hot?"

"Jebber, I reckon there is." Boone said, smiling.

"An' you an' me are gonna go an' find that place, ain't we, Boone?"

"We sure is, Jebber. Now you settle that stoneware good and safe, 'cause we got a ways to travel."

TWELVE

In the late evening glow of the hearth fire, Cassy cuddled the baby, nursing it and humming a sweet melody. Boone lay next to her, stretched out on the pinewood floor, his brain twisting and slithering from one grandiose imagining to another.

"You'll have a fine tailored dress, Cassy. I'll bring one, maybe two or three, back for sure." He seemed to be speaking to the flames in the fire rather than reality. "And somethin' beautiful for new curtains. Some beautiful cloth so's you can make a whole new set of curtains for the whole house. And some books for Chap so's he can learn to read, and…"

"Stop it, Boone," Cassy said, looking hard at her man. "You know we don't need nothin'. We got everything we need right here." She took the baby from her breast and held it up for Boone to see. "Did you ever see such a beautiful child?"

Boone looked at his little son. "No I ain't," he said proudly. " 'Cept for Chap. He was the best thing I ever seen."

"Of course he was. But at long last, after five barren years, this birthin's given us more than a babe. It's a sign."

"A sign of what?" Boone asked as he propped himself up on one elbow.

"Why the rightness of our lives together in this place." Cassy kissed the baby on his peach-fuzz head and held him close to her. "A blessing upon our love, our ways…our land. 'Tis God's good word whispered in our ears, tellin' us to fill this holler with the blood of our kin."

Boone gazed into the fire, the flames almost hypnotizing him. "I ain't against that, Cassy, but right now I got other things on my mind. I need to see what all's out there. I ain't never seen any of the world."

"It can't be better than this," Cassy replied. "We don't lack for nothin'. The crops and the animals feed us more than we can eat. We've got our boys; we've got each other. All our needs are seen to. The sun rises every day and sheds its blessing on us because we live together, all of us, in the truth of the light. And Boone, you know that light is sweet. You know that. You told me that yourself. Standin' in the field with the sun shinin' down on us while we plant our crops, it's the most beautiful thing I know." And then she looked coyly at her man, propped up on his elbow with the light of the fire dancing on his handsome face. "Except for lyin' in your arms with you inside of me," she said as she placed her hand lovingly on his shoulder.

Boone felt the electricity in her touch but even the lure of sex could not bring him back from his imaginings. "I feel the same way, darlin'. But don't you sometimes wonder, away from here, what more there might be?"

"What we got is all we need. I just need you, Boone." She moved her hand from his shoulder to his hair and stroked it gently. "To want for more would be sinful."

Boone shifted ever so slightly, but just enough to pull away from her hand. "That old peddler, he said people should know my name. How do ya reckon that would be? To walk down the street, people pointing, tipping their hat, telling others my name. Sayin' 'Boone Dillard.'"

Cassy rose up from in front of the fireplace and took the baby to its crib in the little room shared with Chap, who was already sound asleep.

"And you'd be at my side, Cassy," Boone said to the fire. "In a fine dress, and we'd just sashay down the street and people would know us. And we'd greet them and say 'howdy do' and, and… maybe we'd have a carriage to ride in, and a driver. Wouldn't that be fine, Cassy? Wouldn't that be just grand?"

Cassy stepped in front of the fire. "I don't need none of that, Boone." She let her dress fall from her body and stood before her man, naked. The firelight silhouetted her hips and the fullness of her breasts, painting her pale flesh in gold. Boone had never seen her look more desirable.

"God almighty, you are a beautiful woman," he said as he began to remove his shirt. Cassy lay down on the rug in front of him, soft and open. "Make love to me, Boone."

He fumbled at the laces of his shoes, stripped off his pants, and stood before her as God had brought him into this world. Then he knelt in front of her and put his hands on her upraised knees and gently spread them apart. "You sure this is all right, Cassy? We ain't done this since the baby came."

"It's all right, Boone. I need you to love me. I need you to just hold me safe."

But before he could move, a loud pounding came at the door.

"Boone! Boone, I need to talk to you," said Jewel from beyond the closed door.

"Lord!" said Boone. "Not now."

Cassy covered herself with her dress. "You'd best talk to her." Boone pulled on his pants and went to the door.

"Jewel, what in all tarnation do you want?" he said as he opened the door.

"Oh, no. I'm sorry," Jewel said as she realized just what she had interrupted. "You two just go ahead."

"Don't be silly, Jewel," Cassy said from across the room. "You go ahead and talk to Boone if you need to."

"Thank you, Cassy. I do need to talk to him," Jewel said as her face flushed with embarrassment.

"Well, let me step outside with you, then, and you can speak your piece," Boone said angrily.

They went out into the field, away from their little homes, and stood under the waning full moon, which was still encircled by tendrils of clouds.

"Boone, there's somethin' I gotta ask," Jewel said with anguish in her voice. "As your sister."

"Go on, then. Gimme a try," Boone said testily.

"It's just…the whole while you're gone, you gotta keep a real close eye on him."

Boone scratched at the dirt with his bare foot. "You know I will, Jewel. But shucks, you should have heard him when we were packin' my wares. 'Boone,' he says to me, 'it's a good thing yer takin' me with you, cause yer not strong like me. If anything bad was to happen, I could get us out of it cause I'm strong. An' without me, why who'd take care of you?'" Boone laughed. "I swear, Jewel, that's what he said to me. He really did."

Panic rose in Jewel's voice. "I am dead *serious*, Boone. He may be big as a bear an' strong as an ox, but when the city folks see him, they gonna take to pullin' his tail."

"They'll sure have their hands full if they try some of that. Jewel," Boone said, laughter rising again in his voice.

"I ain't *jokin'* here, brother." Boone could see the panic in his sister's eyes. "I swear, I got the fear in me, Boone. Jebber may be none too smart, but he knows when folks is pokin' fun at him. You know how riled he can get. And that's when he's gonna need you. 'Cause he ain't meant to live by the same laws as most."

"There's truth in that, all right," Boone said.

Jewel's eyes welled up with tears. "I won't have him gettin' shot. Or caged in some jail." Then she sobbed her deepest fear. "Nor strung up by the neck."

Boone took his little sister into his arms. "Don't you worry none. That won't come to pass, Jewel. I won't let it. I just won't."

Jewel heaved against Boone's chest. "You have to promise me, Boone. I need to hear your word."

He stroked her hair, trying to comfort her. "I promise, Jewel, I won't let no bad come to Jebber."

Boone closed his eyes, and in that instant a vision appeared behind his lids. From the seeing place in his mind Boone saw a crucifix with a figure strapped to it. The figure was that of a naked woman, with her arms outstretched and her legs dangling awkwardly open below her. Boone couldn't quite make out the features of this crucified woman and so he stared at her with a great intensity. The face came into focus and he realized it was his sister Jewel. And she was weeping just as the real Jewel was weeping in his arms.

Embarrassed at seeing his sister naked, Boone blinked his eyes to dispel the image. But instead, the face of the figure changed to that of his wife, Cassy. And she wasn't weeping. She was silent and her eyes were lifeless. Blood flowed from her head and she was like Jesus on the cross.

Boone shuddered and blinked over and over to wipe the terrible vision from his eyes. And gradually, the sight of the crucified Cassy dissolved, and only blackness was left behind Boone's eyelids.

And then, as if to add to the horror, a low eerie chanting came out from the forest, slithering across the field and into Boone's ears. It was dark and guttural and a new shiver of fear coursed Boone's spine. He opened his eyes and thought of the apparition of the night before. Was it back? Had it come for him? He looked to the green wall and saw movement. It *was* back!

Boone unleashed Jewel from his protective embrace and began to move to the field's edge. "Stay put, Jewel. Don't follow me," he said to his sister. "Go back and hold your husband." And he edged closer to the forest as the chanting grew louder, more shrill. A panic had set upon him, but he was determined not to run from it.

"Who's there?" he called. "Come out and show yourself."

The chanting suddenly stopped. Stillness filled the cold night air, absorbing everything into it. And then the green rustled and Boone could see a figure in white moving toward him.

"Come out of those woods," he said again as the panic swirled through him. "Come out, I say."

The figure emerged from the trees, into the field, and Boone saw the object of his fear. It was Delilah, in her nightgown, with what appeared to be a dead snake draped over her shoulders.

"Nana!" cried Boone. "What in devil's name are you doin' there?"

"Tryin' to kill that snake moon," the old woman said. "Before it kills *us*."

Boone looked up and realized that the moon was still girded by the same pale rings as the night before. "It's still there, Nana."

She started to chant again, but the words were unknown to Boone. A language, once spoken on Earth, whose time had long since retreated into the mist. She lifted the dead snake off her shoulders and held it up to the moon. It was a copperhead, six feet long, at least. She sang out a few more words, loudly. Forcefully. Then she threw the snake to the ground and stepped on its reddish head.

"There, you devil of the night," she said. "You leave this family alone." She stomped on it one more time. "Begone!"

Boone looked at the venomous serpent dead on the ground. "How'd you get a copperhead, Nana?"

"I dashed its damn head with a rock."

"Did you have to?" asked Boone. "I don't like killin' nothin' less I have to."

"Boy, that's a snake moon up there," she said. "Your grandfather was bit on the night of a snake moon by a copperhead just like this here. Bit Lem right at the neck whilst he was bent over plantin', just like *you* was gonna do."

She paused, seeing her husband lying in their field, dead. "Night of a snake moon, it was. Nothin' good comes of it, Boone. You have to kill it before it kills you."

Boone put his arm around Delilah. "Don't you worry. I won't let nothin' happen to you."

Delilah pulled away from his embrace. Her eyes filled with tears. "You young fool," she said. "You're goin' away! There ain't nothin' you kin do about what's gonna happen to us here!"

"But Nana…"

"An' there ain't nothin' you kin do about what's gonna happen to *you*, neither," she said. And she fell to her knees, sobbing. Under the snake moon.

THIRTEEN

A smoky blue light hazed off the rolling green hills of the Appalachian range. It was a fine day and Boone and Jebber strode lazily along beside their loaded cart, pulled by a plodding mule. They were somewhere amidst the vast forest of Tennessee, bound for the headwaters that ran north to south out of the mountains, down to Chattanooga, and eventually, down into the great Mississippi River. Boone played a mouth harp as they walked and Jebber hummed along with a tune of his own that bore no relationship to the melody Boone coaxed from his silver Hohner harmonica.

Boone stopped his playing, caught up in a fit of laughter at his brother-in-law. "Jebber, that ain't nowhere near what I'm blowin'. Why don't you hum along with me, so's we can be in tune?"

"What song are you playin', Boone?"

"Camptown ladies."

"Well," Jebber said, "that's the very song I'm hummin'."

Boone just laughed. "Jebber!" he said, shaking his head, and went back to his playing.

The cart moved on through the forest, laden with Boone's pottery, bound for the big city. The two men walked together, secure in each other's company.

"Ain't nothin' gonna happen to us, Boone," Jebber said. "Not as long as I'm with you."

Boone smiled at the strong man-boy. "I know that, Jebber. You'll watch out for me, won't you?"

"You bet I will, Boone. An' Jewel said you'd watch out for me, too."

"That I will, Jebber. That I will." Boone thought for a bit. "She didn't want you to go, did she?"

Jebber shook his head from side to side. "Nope," he said. Then he realized what Boone had asked. "How'd you know that?"

"I just did," Boone said.

"But I told her I had to see big city," Jebber added. "An' then she said okay." He reached down to pluck a wild buttercup from the forest floor, smelled it, and tucked it behind his ear. " 'Course, that was after I loved her up. She said fer me, just don't get us in no trouble, that's all."

"Cassy didn't want me to go, neither. Grandma, too." Boone saw some wild mint, plucked a few leaves, rolled them into a little tube, and put them between his cheek and gums. He sucked at the tube and it was clean and fresh in his mouth. "Seems nobody wanted us to go."

" 'Cept us!" Jebber said.

"You're right, there, Jebber," Boone smiled at his big bodyguard. "And where we goin'?"

"We's goin' to big city! *Hoo-whee!*"

The mule responded to Jebber's cry of joy with a *heehaw* of its own. The men both laughed, and the sound they made mingled with the mule, and the three of them "*heehawed*" into the fine spring air, somewhere in the middle of the East Tennessee Appalachian Mountains. In beguilement, the three settled down and walked on in silence, with only the song of the birds of the forest and the creaky roll of the cartwheels to accompany them.

Finally Jebber had to speak. "When we gonna git there, Boone?"

"Well, we ain't there yet," Boone said.

Jebber was getting antsy. "We been gone two days now, an' we ain't nowhere."

"Sure we are, Jebber. We're in the forest." Boone spread his arms wide. "We're in God's green wilderness. The forest that covers everything, I reckon. Except where men have cleared it away to make farms and towns. 'Cept for those, it's all forest, everywhere." They moved on, through the green, and Boone's mind thought of things to come. "You know, Jebber, I reckon this here country of ours, this here America, will be forests forever. We'll be a country of farms and towns with the green woods all around us. And we'll be livin' in harmony with the cycles of life.

That's what I imagine the future holds for the state of Tennessee, and our nation of these United States of America."

"But Boone," Jebber said, "what about that war that's goin' on? Men is killin' each other because of what the coloreds did."

"The coloreds ain't done nothin', you fool. They just want their freedom. Any man has a right to that."

"Then what's the killin' about?" Jebber asked, unable to grasp the nature of war.

Boone pondered the question for a moment. "Well, I reckon it's about greed," he said. "Men kill each other for the want of things. I reckon the South wants to keep the coloreds as slaves, workin' the land, pickin' the cotton."

"That don't seem like no kind of harmony to me," Jebber said.

"It ain't," Boone responded. "They's planted too much of one crop. You can't do that. You got to mix it up with different crops to keep the soil happy. They's planted too much cotton and they have to use the coloreds to pick the cotton." Boone sucked his mint roll and spat on the ground. "Hell, them slaves work for free. They do all the work and they don't get nothin' back. Nothin' of the land is theirs."

Jebber understood. "That ain't right. No wonder they wants their freedom. I wouldn't work fer nothin' neither. No man should."

Boone nodded his head at Jebber's innate wisdom. "And that, I reckon, is what the killin' is all about."

"I hope we don't see no killin'," Jebber shuddered.

"Don't you worry," Boone said reassuringly to his man-boy bodyguard. "We ain't got nothin' to fight nobody over. We's just goin' to Chattanooga to sell my wares. We ain't gonna see no war."

At that instant, the brush exploded with an unleashed fury. A streak of yellow burst out of the dense undergrowth and hurled itself at the mule. A mountain lion, flashing its fangs, ripped and tore at the yoked beast's throat. The mule, braying insanely, fell back on its haunches from the fury of the attack. It was hopeless. The life draining quickly out of the poor beast. Boone shouted at the killer, but the cat was crazed, bent on the blood of an easy kill. It was not afraid of the men, as if some malevolence had possessed the great cat and removed all its natural inhibitions.

Boone kept on shouting and stomping to no avail as the cat stuck its canines deeper into the mule's throat. Jebber drew his sling blade and swung wildly at the mountain lion, slashing it across its rear haunches. The cat shrieked with pain, withdrawing its fangs from the mule's jugular. It spun around and challenged Jebber, snarling and flashing its teeth. Jebber swung again and caught the cat on its front paw. The attacker gave one last shriek of rage and bolted off into the forest, disappearing into the green. Jebber ran after it for a few loping strides, then rushed back to the bloodied mule, tears flowing down his cheeks.

"Boone, do somethin'!" he cried out. "Do somethin' quick, she's hurt real bad."

Boone only stood there, shaking his head in disgust. "Ain't nothin' to be done, Jebber."

Jebber knelt beside the mule, gently stroking her muzzle. "We gots to mend her," he sobbed. "We gots to fix her good and leave her to rest."

Boone put a hand on Jebber's shoulder. "It's hopeless, Jebber. And ain't two ways about it. If that ol' mule don't pull this cart, you do."

That caught Jebber's attention and stirred him from his grief. He looked at Boone, then back at the animal. He grabbed the beast by the ears and pulled her up on both shanks. Blood flowed from the mule's neck and mouth as crimson foam spewed from her nostrils.

"Git up, mule," Jebber shouted. "Git along, now, ya hear! Git!" He slammed the mule with a boot to her rump and the mule collapsed, blowing one last bloody snort in the dust. Dead.

FOURTEEN

Thick, dark clouds dappled the blue sky over Coker Creek Hollow. The wind blew through the trees making the leaves shudder and the grass bend to its power. Cassy was in a meadow, gathering berries, as the coming storm began to creep up from the southwest.

Her basket was almost filled with the small, wild strawberries of the spring. She moved through pockets of light and shadow, bending to her knees and plucking the ripe red fruit from the brambles. She was humming to herself, trying to drown out the fearful voices that chattered in her mind. The voices that told her that Boone was gone, and would never come back to her. And that he would run off with another woman and she would never see him again. She didn't want to believe those voices and yet she heard them, taunting her, and she wished she had made love to Boone on their last night together. And they would have, she thought, if it hadn't of been for that fool sister of his, and Jewel's worries about that big, dumb Jebber. When Boone finally came back to her that night she had already fallen asleep. And the next morning Boone was in no mood for lovemaking. And so the voices assailed her with accusations, telling her lies that just might be true.

She reached down to pick a final cluster of berries and a shadow fell upon her. But it was not from the dark clouds. It was a man's shadow.

Cassy, on her knees, looked up and saw a wild bearded man hovering over her. He was blackened with the smoke and grime of battle, and he was wearing a ragged blue uniform of the Union Army. It was a Yankee, with captain's bars on his tattered collar.

Cassy cried out at the terrible sight of him.

"No need for that, little lady," he said in a voice that sounded as ragged as he appeared. He drew his saber and Cassy thought surely he was going to kill her. But he put the tip of his steel under her chin and forced her to rise to her feet. "Ain't you a pretty little thing, then," he said. His lips parted with a jagged-toothed leer, his eyes ravaged with war.

Cassy trembled, her limbs shaking with fear. The captain moved the sword to Cassy's neck and she thought he was going to plunge it into her, taking her life in one insane thrust. Instead, he used the tip to pop the top button of her dress. And then he moved down, button by button, to her waist. The dress fell to Cassy's hips, exposing her swollen bosom. The captain caught up a gasp of air at the sight of her soft, white flesh.

"Oh my Lord," he said. He brushed the blade against her breasts, tracing circles around her areolas, and he grinned again. "Lord a' mercy, this is one fine day for pluckin' juicy berries." The sword's edge scraped her distended nipple. "You got milk in those teats?" Cassy, frozen with fear, nodded. Her eyes were wet with tears. "That's good," the captain said, " 'cause I sure could use a drink. I'm parched somethin' wicked."

The captain fell upon her, pressing his grubby, whiskered face to Cassy's breasts, and began to suck greedily. Cassy could only stand there, staring out at the green forest, the voices squealing in her head. And then she saw them. A small band of soldiers all dressed in Yankee blue, stepping out from the trees. There were eight, maybe ten, all dark with the filth of war, bloodied and bandaged. And they were all hungry.

FIFTEEN

Boone and Jebber had passed down out of the hills onto a sloping plain. And, sure enough, Jebber was pulling the cart, slogging through mud raised by a steady spring rain. It fell with the softness of fresh water, rinsing all creation, cleansing the earth. But rain couldn't cleanse the madness that was upon the land in the year of 1863.

"Boone," Jebber said from between the shafts, "that dang cat tore at our mule's neck. An' you told me Nana's husband was killed by a copperhead what bit his neck, too."

Boone sloshed alongside his brother-in-law as the cart struggled through the mire. "That's right, Jebber."

"Why they always go fer the neck?" Jebber asked.

"I suppose it's the jugular they're after." Boone pondered a bit. "How you pull that load and talk all at the same time is beyond me."

Jebber laughed. " 'Cause I'm strong, Boone. You know that."

The rain continued to fall, soaking the earth and all that was upon it. The two men moved through the wetness, pulling their load of treasure, moving toward their fate.

"Jug'ler?" Jebber asked. "What's that?"

"It's like a river of blood," Boone said, "flowin' from the heart straight to the brain. The animals know if they strike there, they're sure to get a kill. Know it by instinct."

"In stink?" Jebber said.

"Yep. It's like...they just know. It's like...they catch the smell of death, and they strike."

Jebber shook with a shiver, the water jumping off of him like a dog out of a pond. "What do ya reckon that stink smells like?"

Boone stopped and tilted his head, listening. "Shush, Jebber. I hear something."

Jebber trundled along, the faithful beast hauling his load. "What is it, Boone?"

Boone darted rapidly ahead, bounding up a rocky ridge, leaving Jebber behind.

"Don't leave me here alone!" Jebber shouted.

Boone scrambled up the rise, stopped, and peered out into the wilderness. "I knew it. Water!" He turned and shouted back at his man-mule. "I hear water, Jebber!"

Jebber muttered to himself, venting his ire at hauling the cart. "Been pourin' rain since noon an' *now* he hears water. An' he's supposed to be the smart one."

Jebber gently set the cart shafts to the wet ground and stepped out from between them. He lumbered forward, trailing Boone who moved up the rise, chasing higher ground. Jebber finally caught up and the two seekers stood side-by-side atop a small promontory. Boone pointed through the trees. "There, ya see?" he said.

Down below, through the murk and the timber, was a river. A roiling, angry river. Swollen by the spring melt of winter's snows. Roaring its power to the world.

Jebber was shaken to the quick. "Aw, Boone…"

"That's it, Jebber!" Boone cried happily. "That's it!"

Jebber turned away, not bearing to look anymore. "Oh, Boone. No, I can't."

Boone looked quizzically at his partner. "What's vexin' you now, Jebber? That river's what we been huntin'."

Jebber was silent. Then his fear seeped out, up from his belly and across his tongue. "Boone…that river…it sounds like death smells."

SIXTEEN

The rain that fell on Boone and Jebber was now falling on the Dillard farm in Coker Creek Hollow. The gloomy dusk bore little light, but from within Boone's home came unruly laughter and bawdy singing, candlelight spilling from every window.

Inside Boone's sanctuary, Cassy, Jewel, and Delilah had fed the Yankees pork and biscuits and root vegetables. The ragged, starving men had eaten virtually the entire hog that Chap had slaughtered, and devoured most of the store of provisions that Boone and Cassy had laid up. Now, they were working on Boone's corn liquor, and they were getting sloppy.

Cassy and Jewel tried to stay busy, collecting dishware and tidying up. Hoping the men would pass out before their hunger moved from their bellies to their groins. Cassy had been thoroughly humiliated by the captain and she did not want things to go any further. Delilah sat in a rocking chair, comforting the baby, Chap at her side. The boy, like all boys, was fascinated by the soldiers, even if they were a filthy, shiftless lot. He saw their weapons of blue steel, their leather holsters, their uniforms, and he was mesmerized.

The men passed the jug, taking long draughts, and sang songs from the North that the women had never heard before. Songs of war and songs of the women back home that they would someday return to. And then lewd, obscene songs, accompanied by roaring laughter that made Cassy and Jewel fearful.

One young soldier was still eating. He was a big, pimply faced private whose right arm ended in a stump just below the shoulder. The wound was swathed in bandages, soiled with dirt and black blood. He worked awkwardly with the fork in his left hand, but at last he finished up. Cassy bent over the boy to take his plate and the private's one good arm snaked itself around her waist.

"I hanker for a drink," the one-armed boy said.

Cassy gestured to the jug being passed amongst the soldiers. "What we got is in that jug."

The private leered a buck-toothed smile. "My taste is for a suck like the captain had."

Cassy tried to pull away, but the arm held her tight.

The captain saw what was happening. "Private Van Pelt, not here." His whiskered chin jutted toward Delilah and the baby. "Besides, truth be told, her milk's rancid as a dead goat's." He laughed, and the drunken men joined him, cackling with a foul oafishness. The women were made afraid by the animal sound of the soldiers' laughter.

"Excuse me, Captain," the private said as his one good arm pulled Cassy close to him. "I'm obliged to take her outside, and my mind's set. Less 'a course you object, sir."

The captain looked at the poor wretch of a youth. "God knows, son, you've paid your price."

The private smiled up at Cassy. "And with milk, ain't nothin' like a piece 'a pie."

"Y'all ate what we got prepared," Cassy said, not catching the drift of the private's remark.

The soldier's hand quickly uncoiled from around Cassy's waist and shot up under her dress, groping at her crotch. "The slice I'm after is right here," he said. "All it needs is a little warmin' up."

The drunken men laughed raucously. And in one swift move, the private hoisted Cassy up over his shoulder as he rose to his feet. He moved to the door, carrying her like a sack of potatoes.

Jewel, her eyes blazing with fear and anger, grabbed a kitchen knife and lunged toward the one-armed oaf. "You bastard!" she screamed.

The captain leapt from his chair and grabbed Jewel's wrist before she could plunge her blade into her quarry. He twisted it harshly, forcing the kitchen knife to fall to the floor. "No need to pitch a fit, sweetcakes, there's plenty 'a fun to go around." Then he whispered in her ear. "For *all* the boys."

The private, with Cassy over his shoulder kicking and

screaming, slipped out the door into the wet darkness, off to the barn.

SEVENTEEN

Boone and Jebber stood at the river's edge. It was the great Tennessee River that they had come to. It was smooth and wide rather than the monster they had first seen.

"See here?" Boone said. "Away from them falls, she's just a big, ol' flat river. Ain't no cause for alarm, Jebber."

Jebber was not reassured, even though the rain had let up. His gaze drifted off the water and into the sky. Wind-whipped clouds, snaky and black, encircled what was left of the moon. Strangling it.

"That the same moon as back home?" Jebber asked.

"Sure 'nough," Boone replied. "Don't matter where you go in this world, there ain't but one."

As Boone spoke, the clouds completely blotted out the moon. There seemed no light anywhere on Heaven or Earth. And then, a glowing globe appeared—but sitting low in the sky—and it appeared to be moving, floating, as if it were a moon of some other world. And it was being slowly drawn toward Boone and Jebber.

And in the approach of that eerie light, Boone saw what appeared to be the shrouded face of death. A fear clutched his chest and squeezed for a moment. But then it released its grip. For as death came closer, Boone saw it was only a man, his face poking from the cowl of a rain slicker, his ossified hands holding a long pole; but his flesh was aglimmer as if phosphorescent. He was a boatman, poling his craft through the mist hovering low on the river, a fiery orange lantern hanging at the prow.

Boone, relieved, cried out, "Hey there! Boatman!"

The cowled figure heard the call from the bank and maneuvered his flat-bottomed barge to shore, coming up to Boone and Jebber and their pottery-laden cart.

Jebber's eyes bugged out as the deathly figure stepped from the front of the craft that had come aground at their feet. "Mister, you are white as a ghost!"

The boatman sank a trident-shaped anchor into the mud, securing his barge. "I been haulin' lime for the graves," he said in a voice that seemed to come almost from beyond him. A voice that said he had seen things that had removed him from ordinary reality. And he would never be the same. "The wind kicked up, covered me like baker's flour 'fore I could get the tarp battened down."

"You a ferryman?" Boone asked.

"I'm that, too," the boatman answered. "Mostly I grind limestone, take it where there's need."

"There's money in that?"

"No better livin' than the dyin'. One time or another, every man, woman, an' child's a customer."

"And I don't reckon many come back for seconds," Boone joked.

The boatman sniggered a raspy cackle. "Where you boys lookin' to git?"

"We're goin' to big city," Jebber said.

"I seen a lot of them, son. They ain't no different from anywhere else." He coughed up a gob of phlegm and spat on the ground. " 'Cept they's worse."

"Well, we're gonna sell Boone's wares in big city!"

"Then the Lord protect you fools. Don't you know there's a war on?"

"We heard of it," Boone said. "But we ain't seen none of it."

"Maybe the war's a ghost like you are," Jebber said.

The boatman sniggered again and shook his head, disbelieving. "I'm headed to Chattanooga, and I'm open to yer trade."

"What's the price," Boone asked.

"Silver coin," the boatman replied. "That's all I trust."

Boone wagged a thumb at his cart. "All I got is my wares."

The cowled figure looked Boone up and down, as if appraising his worth. "Fair enough, son. There's other ways to settle accounts."

EIGHTEEN

The one-armed, pimple-faced private ran into the barn with his spoils of war slung over his shoulder. He dumped Cassy onto a pile of straw and kneeled, straddling her. He drew a bayonet from his bootleg. "I ain't fixin' to hurt you," he said. "I'm hopin' you'll come to like it. And this bein' my first time with the one arm…I could do with your help."

He hesitated, as if waiting for a response, but Cassy gave none. She stared blankly beyond him, out the barn door and into the blackness that had engulfed her. The rain continued to fall.

The private, with the bayonet in hand, realized he was helpless to go any further. Frustration crept over him, and he spat his words at Cassy. "Shit, woman. Go ahead! Tug down my britches."

Cassy was frozen, unable to move in the darkness that was coiling around her. And then he struck her. Hard, beside the ear, with the hilt of the bayonet. "I ain't got the patience of Job!" he screamed.

Cassy came out of her fog, the side of her head shrieking with pain. Her hands began to move involuntarily, and her fingers, as if they had a consciousness of their own, reached up and fumbled at the private's belt.

A flash of lightning threw a great lamp over the Dillard farm. Calcium white light streamed through the open barn door, casting the shadow of a small boy against the wall above Cassy and her tormentor. The shadow held an axe, raised high.

The private, seeing the boy's cast image, spun around, slipping to one side of Cassy, his blade thrust out in front of him. But it was too late. The axe fell. Burning the air past the tormentor's head and tearing into his good shoulder, cutting clean his one good arm.

For the briefest moment, the private was silent, totally numb. He looked down at his limbless torso, blood pumping from his freshly severed stump, and then he unleashed a blood-curdling scream. Chap grasped a handful of the private's long, matted hair to steady his shrieking head and expose his throbbing neck. With every ounce of strength in his child's frame, he wielded a one-handed wild swing and slashed the private's head clean off his body.

Inside Boone's home, the captain and the men heard the scream and came rushing out the cabin door. They stumbled drunkenly toward the barn. Cassy and Chap, running hand-in-hand, raced across the newly planted field, heading for the green wall of trees. Once there, they would be safe in the forest. They could disappear into the darkness of nature.

But at that instant, the rain clouds parted and the waning snake moon lit the field with a sickly, milky light. The captain saw the pair, sloshing through the spring wetness. He pulled a thin, black cheroot from his mouth and tossed it on the ground, unholstered his sidearm, raised it, and drew a tight bead on the fleeing figures. The pistol exploded. A slug of whirling lead hurtled across the field and slammed into the back of Cassy's skull. The bullet ripped through her brain, tearing away all consciousness, obliterating all feeling, and sending Cassy into the arms of her creator. She fell like a slaughtered ox, her head a bloody, pulpy mass. Chap stopped, screamed, "Mommy!" and then darted off, zigzagging through the field. Before the captain could draw another bead, the boy was through the green wall and gone.

The captain blew smoke from the hot barrel, then reholstered his gun. "Got one, anyways," he said. The men laughed and, without bothering to ascertain the fate of their beheaded comrade, turned back to the cabin to find Jewel just as they'd left her: stripped naked, bound at the wrists and ankles, spread-eagled to the posts of the bed in Boone and Cassy's room. It would be a long night, as they'd each take their turn, then fall back into ranks, waiting for another.

NINETEEN

Jebber and Boone had rolled their treasure-laden cart up two planks that the boatman had lowered across the low gunwale of his barge, and the craft pushed off into the mottled darkness. Jebber had never been on a river before, and was unsteady on his feet as the barge rocked along on the oily, black water.

"I don't believe I much take to boats," Jebber said.

Boone lifted his fists in front of the lamp, entwined his hands, and raised two fingers straight up. Like magic, the shadow of a rabbit appeared in the spill of light fluttering on the river. "Jebber," Boone said, "even little ol' Mister Bunny ain't afraid of this little creek. Hell, betcha it ain't deeper than your knees."

Jebber giggled like a child, watching raptly as Boone's bunny hippity-hopped over the swirling flow of the Tennessee River.

The boatman passed before the lantern, coiling his anchor rope. His shrouded figure blotted out the joyous antics of the hand puppet. The rabbit disappeared as the white-faced man just stood there, absorbing all the light.

Jebber let out a low moan. "Awww, the bunny's gone."

Boone looked up into the man's stark-white face. In the lamplight, the quick-lime powder gave off a sickly incandescence. "Mister," Boone said, "how is it you seen us, yet we lit no fire, nor nothin'?"

The boatman peered at Boone, but his eyes seemed to have no pupils. There was light on his face but only empty black sockets where his eyes should have been. Or so it appeared to Boone.

"I'm like a bat," the cowled figure said. "My eyes cut the dark. It's the light blinds my vision."

A jagged bolt of lightning creased the sky. The boatman's head jerked up river as a booming thunderclap followed close on the heels of the flash of light. Jebber cried out in fear.

"You best lash down yer cart," the boatman said. "Looks like a might choppy, up yonder."

Boone looked ahead, and another flash of lightning lit a rip in the river. The water crushed through a narrow, rocky flume, angry white spray mixing with the black mist.

"Sweet Jesus!" Boone said.

The thunder boomed again. Jebber, terrified, squatted on his haunches, arms circling his knees, hugging them tight to his chest.

"Boone!" he cried out. "I wanna go home. I don't wanna go to big city. Take me home, Boone. Take me home, right now."

Boone unspooled rope from the ship's capstan. He rapidly fashioned a lasso and ringed it around Jebber's chest. Cinching it tight, he said, "Jebber, you just hold fast to this rope. Don't let go. Never!" Then he worked frantically, running lengths of rope to the cart, securing them to cleats on all sides of the barge. The river was now rushing furiously and the craft was being swept along with it, almost completely out of control. The lightning again ripped a jagged crack in the black sky, illuminating the enraged river. Boone saw a huge boulder looming dead ahead. Scared witless, he cried to the boatman, but his scream of warning was drowned out by another blast of thunder that seemed to explode its fury just above his head. Jebber wailed with terror. The barge slammed broadside into the boulder, launching itself upright as if being shot for the moon. The boatman, clinging astern to the rudder, his face lit like a demon in the depths of Hell, cackled an insane laughter like some madman at the wheel of his own *Pequod*.

"Boone!" Jebber shouted in terror, "save us!"

TWENTY

Jewel lay on the bed, weeping, as Delilah cut her free from her bonds. The soldiers had gone, slinking off before sunup after satisfying their needs. The captain had tossed a gold piece onto Jewel's stomach as he left, his parting words: "I wouldn't want you to think you worked all night for nothin', sweetcakes."

Delilah could hear the men laughing like pigs as they receded into the woods. "Don't pay no mind to nothin', Jewel. Nothin' happened to you." She covered Jewel with a blanket as the violated young woman clutched the gold piece tightly in her hand, squeezing it as if to somehow crush out the pain she felt enveloping her heart. And she began to heave with sobs.

"I ain't no good fer nothin' now, Nana," Jewel said through her tears. "They ruined me. They ruined me fer my Jebber."

"No they ain't, girl. I'm tellin' you, nothin' happened." Delilah stroked Jewel's forehead. "It was just a nightmare you had. A bad dream like you had when you were a child."

Jewel shook her head maniacally. Her eyes were wide with panic. A horror was sweeping through her, making Delilah's words meaningless. She was retreating into herself, into a numbness that would not allow for any feeling or any reflection on what had happened.

"I ain't no good fer Jebber now!" she cried out in her anguish. "I might as well just follow them soldiers and let them ruin me completely." She looked into Delilah's eyes, and the old woman saw that the light was going out of them. Jewel could feel herself falling into a blackness from which there was no exit. She was being sucked into a hole that tunneled out on the other end into madness. She was losing her hold on reality, and in her mind she was becoming worthless. In her mind she was nothing but a whore.

She held out the gold coin to Delilah. "Look, Nana. They paid me."

Delilah stroked the wretched girl's head. "Hush now, Jewel. You be still and rest yerself. You had bad dreams, was all, and yer havin' more now."

But Jewel was beyond comforting. "They paid me!" she cried out. "I'm a girl that can work for her living." The light receded further from her eyes. "I don't just give it away. I make money doin' it, Nana."

"You stop that, Jewel," Delilah scolded. "I'm goin' out to git Cassy and Chap. Hopefully nothin' happened to her with that one-armed Yankee."

She swooped up the baby and went out the door. Jewel just lay there, staring at the ceiling, her mind swirling with demons that howled their filth at her, shaming her. And her heart went numb.

Then she heard Delilah's cry, coming from the newly planted field. "Oh my Lord! No!"

TWENTY-ONE

A smoky black fog blanketed the wide, swollen river. The barge had made it through the hellish chasm and the water was now flat, the current tailing slowly. A glint of moonbeam slipped through the clouds and Jebber—all alone and still lassoed to the barge's capstan—saw a paddleboat steamer up ahead. But the steamer was still as death in the quiet water, battered and beached upon a ragged shoal.

The boatman's barge drifted slowly past the wrecked stern-wheeler and nothing aboard the big boat moved. Jebber, lying on his belly, clinging to the safety rope with both hands, called over the low gunwale to the wreck. "Hallooo. Anybody out there!" Then he looked back, up and down the barge. "Boone! Where are you?" But there was no reply, and a terror settled upon Jebber.

Finally a voice called out. A reassuring voice. And the fear that was in Jebber fell away. "What you callin' to, Jebber?" Boone asked as he crawled out from under the box of the cart.

"I thought I was all alone, Boone," Jebber said, breaking into a relieved smile. "I thought you'd left me here to die."

Boone stretched himself, looking about to get his bearings, then shuffled across the deck. He crouched beside the big man-boy and put a comforting hand on his trembling shoulder.

"We made it, buddy," Boone said. "We done got out with our skins."

"I was so scared, Boone. But I'm better now."

Boone slapped Jebber hard on the back of his head.

"*Oww!* Don't be doin' me like that, Boone."

Boone laughed out into the last blackness of the night. "Jebber, that's the way you make the fear skedaddle. Ghosts, too."

"You just hit someone upside the head?" Jebber asked as he rubbed the back of his neck. "That makes ghosts go away?"

Boone laughed again. "Ghosts is only in people's heads."

"Oh, yeah? Well, where's that boatman at?" Jebber asked.

Boone pointed to the wrecked steamer slowly drifting away. "Maybe he's on that stern-wheeler." He sucked his cheeks and spat over the gunwale into the river. " 'Cause he sure as hell ain't here."

"Where'd he go then?" Jebber asked again.

"I reckon the Lord took him," Boone said. "Or maybe the devil." And he began to loosen Jebber from his harness. "Now let's get you outta that rope, Jebber. 'Cause you and me's got to guide this here barge all the way to Chattanooga."

Free of his restraint, Jebber shook himself like a marionette, loosening his tightened muscles. "I ain't afraid of nothin' no more." And he shook himself free of the terrors of the night. Then he shouted out, "And we's goin' to big city! *Hoo-whee!*"

TWENTY-TWO

The barge drifted lazily along. Boone was slouched over the rudder and Jebber was sprawled on the foredeck. They were both sound asleep.

An unseasonable heat had come after the rain. A ridge of high pressure had moved over eastern Tennessee, driving the storm off to North Carolina where it worked its way out to the Atlantic Ocean. It was a hot red sun that slowly crept into the sky, erasing the blackness of the night. A thin flush of daylight began to break the mist on the river. The whippoorwills began the song of the morning, calling to each other from opposite riverbanks. They were soon joined by yellow warblers, scarlet tanagers, black and white warblers, and a myriad of song sparrows. The green vegetation came to life with melody and the pileated woodpeckers struck up a rhythmic accompaniment as they hammered tree bark, searching for fresh spring grubs and mites. It was another fine morning, and Boone and Jebber slept like the dead.

It had been two days since they had lost the boatman. Boone had piloted the craft down river, but the languid current left them with little to do. The barge seemed to propel itself, drifting at a hypnotic pace through the green Tennessee wilderness. The life of the natural world engulfed them, fed by the great river, and spring had brought a glorious explosion of lushness to the earth, awakening everything from winter's hibernation.

But Boone was oblivious to it all. He was taking his pottery to Chattanooga and he was going to sell it for more money than he had ever thought possible. He was going to be rich. And perhaps even more important, he was going to be famous. And so he dreamed, asleep at the rudder, of things that were far beyond the good life he led at Coker Creek Hollow.

As the day began to blossom, the shallow-draft barge approached the fork of the Tennessee and Chickamauga Rivers, and as the fates would have it, the pilotless craft slipped off course, down the Chickamauga, where a bitter cup awaited Boone Dillard and Jebber Stubbs.

Drifting into a backwater eddy—beneath a tangled canopy of giant cypress and Spanish moss, the banks lined with river birch and Southern cane and swamp oak—the barge moved slowly into the approaching heat of the day. Boone stirred from the delusions of his dream, wakened to the glorious morning, and stretched himself in the dappled light.

Something floating in the murky water hit the boat. A hollow wooden thud, then another, and yet one more. Jebber roused from his slumber.

"Boone, what's out there?" he called.

Both men peered into the mist still hovering low on the river. Then a breeze rustled the trees and revealed the source of the thuds. Coffins. Pinewood caskets. Dozens of them, bobbing in the muddy, edgewater flow. Jebber stood close behind Boone, fearfully looking over his shoulder.

"Thy Lord," Boone said into the morning air. "What is this we've come to?"

The barge was surrounded by caskets. Clean and fresh and newly sawn and nailed to hold the mortal remains of the warriors of the War Between the States.

A thunderous rumble rolled up the river. Boom after boom. It was cannon fire, but the sound was unknown to Jebber and Boone. They gazed downstream.

"That another storm heading our way?" Jebber asked.

Boone was puzzled. "I ain't never heard thunder like that. Don't see no lightnin', neither."

"Maybe in these here parts, things is different from what we know," Jebber said.

Boone looked up, through the canopy of cypress and Spanish moss, to the high, clear sky above. "There ain't even no clouds, Jebber. How in God's name could there be thunder?"

Jebber's eyes were on the coffins. "Boone! Looky thar!"

Another coffin had cut their path, but this one was crushed

open, the pine lid torn off. Stretched out inside was a Yankee cavalry officer, his plumed hat propped upon his chest, his glistening sword grasped in the rigid fingers of one hand. Below the tails of his gold-braided blue coat, two bloody stumps protruded. It all became clear to Boone.

"By damn, man," he said. "That peddler wasn't just airin' his lungs." Boone swept forth his hand, gesturing at the floating caskets. They's *all* soldiers."

Jebber reached out and grabbed hold of the coffin. He snatched the hat from the dead man's chest.

"Hoo-whee!" I never did see such a fancy-pants hat!" He propped the hat atop his head, then tugged the sword from the corpse's death grip. He ripped the air with a fast succession of swings, thrusts, and parries. "Hoo-whee!" the man-boy shouted out, his eyes wide with fascination—the entrancement of all boys for all things military. "This is right fine things, Boone."

But Boone's thoughts were elsewhere. He looked across the bobbing coffins, an armada of the dead in a backwater of the Chickamauga River, as the cannonry continued to roar.

"By fire and God," he whispered. "What kind of place *is* this?"

TWENTY-THREE

It was a warm, clear morning at Coker Creek Hollow. Puffs of cottony clouds drifted high in the sky. The song sparrows and warblers and finches sang out their morning melody into the sweetness of the spring air. The flowering dogwood trees and the cherry trees, the pawpaw trees and the peach trees were bursting with flowers. The chickens in the henhouse clucked happily as they went about their task of egg laying. The huge Poland-China sow was contentedly suckling her piglets. The milk cow was chewing her cud, waiting to be unburdened of her weight of morning milk. And Delilah, Jewel, and Chap had just dug a grave for Cassy.

It was up a rise, behind Boone's house, in the shade of the limbs of an old, black hickory tree overlooking their homestead. Overlooking the little hollow that was almost paradise.

"She can watch everything from here," Delilah said. "She can look down on us and share in everything we do." Delilah hugged Chap. "Yer ma will always be with us, Chap. And she loved you more than anything in the world. You always remember that, you hear me?"

The boy began to shed his sorrow and his loss. "She's dead, Nana," he said through a rush of tears. "And I miss her so much."

Delilah stroked his head, softly and gently. "I know you do, Chap. We all do."

The old woman stretched an arm out to Jewel and drew her to her bosom, holding her tight against Chap. And there they stood, the three of them arms around each other, locked in embrace, weeping for the loss of their beloved Cassy. They stood beside a

82 · RAY MANZAREK

hole in the ground with a shrouded body lying next to it.

"Nana," Jewel finally said, "I'll be leaving here as soon as we cover over Cassy."

Delilah looked into Jewel's eyes, but the light had not come back into them. "Why, girl? Where will you go?"

"I don't know," Jewel said as she moved back from their embrace. "But I ain't no good for Jebber. Not anymore. Not after what they done to me." She stepped to the feet of the shrouded figure. "Help me, here. Let's get poor Cassy in the ground."

And when they finished filling the grave and mounding the dirt, Delilah placed a cross of twisted dogwood upon it. "They say Jesus was crucified on a cross of dogwood," Delilah said. "And this day we do send you off to paradise, Cassy, to rejoin Jesus in the light."

"Amen," said Jewel.

"I love you, Mommy," Chap said as he fell to his knees at the graveside.

Jewel touched Chap's head lovingly, and walked off. Down the hill. Away from Coker Creek Hollow.

TWENTY-FOUR

Squatting astern, Boone guided the keelboat down the center of the slow-moving channel. Jebber wore the plumed hat on his head and held the sword aloft, poised at the prow like a gallant swashbuckler. Childish delusions of grandeur chased after each other in Jebber's brain, the brain of an eight-year-old. It was a lazy afternoon, hot and clear, and a time for daydreaming.

Then Boone sighted something in the distance—a swirling cloud, much like a dust devil, rising from the berm that ran above the river's edge. And out of that smoky whirlwind, a gleaming, richly lacquered horse-drawn coach rattled forth. It was drawn by a pitch-black stallion and the carriage itself was pearlescent white with golden filigrees encircling the windows and doors.

"Jebber, I reckon we're just about there," Boone said.

The swashbuckler looked ahead. "I don't see no big city," Jebber replied.

"Not on the river, up there on the bank." Boone pointed to the whirlwind. "You see that rig comin' off yonder?"

Jebber nodded. "Yep. Now I see it."

Boone laughed with delight. "She looks to be slicker than a wet fish. You won't find no cart like that lessen you's by a big city, or somethin'." He cut the rudder hard and the barge veered toward the bank.

As it edged up against the shoreline, Jebber hopped off the boat and scrambled up the scarp to the roadway. He stood in the path of the oncoming carriage, waving his cavalry hat for the coach to stop.

A black man, in black livery, reined in the stallion, bringing the lacquered coach to an abrupt halt just before it ran over Jebber.

83

The man-boy bowed with a flourish and placed his plumed hat back on his head.

"Thankee fer stoppin'," Jebber said to the driver. "Is big city where y'all came from? Is it back up the road?"

The driver didn't say a word, he merely gestured a thumb back at the coach. Jebber moved around the great black beast pulling the carriage and to the gilded door at the side of the vehicle. He tapped at the curtained window. The red velvet behind the glass parted and Jebber saw the lily-white face of a young lady peering out at him. And she was the most beautiful woman Jebber had ever seen.

He stepped back, almost reverently, removed his hat, bowed his head, and said, "Sorry, ma'am." It was as if Jebber had understood something about the face in the window. Something unapproachable, almost otherworldly. He instinctively knew he should not press himself upon her. His child's mind knew that he was too crude and rough for her innate elegance. The notion of purity entered Jebber's mind for the first time in his life, and he was awestruck at the revelation. And for a moment, as he starred at her, everything was suspended in time.

Then Boone came bounding up to Jebber's side, bringing with him a return to the here and now. The soft blue eyes of the beautiful woman behind the glass saw Boone's handsome face, and behind that face, his surety, his inner strength. The carriage door opened to him.

And Boone saw her. He saw the whiteness of her skin and the delicacy of her aristocratic features. Her high cheekbones and the red fullness of her lips. The ringlets of golden hair that fell about her shoulders in a waterfall of softness. The embroidered dress of an impossibly white silk with a plunging décolleté that exposed the barest hint of cleavage—a hint that promised delights beyond anything a country man had ever dreamed.

Then this radiant creature stepped out of the carriage. Her movements were slow and graceful. She seemed to glide in the air, as if she were not connected to the earth at all. She came up to Boone and their eyes met. He could not speak, for her beauty had thunderstruck him. And he felt himself falling into her eyes. Her blue eyes looked into his and pulled Boone out of himself, into a place he had never before been. He was enraptured by her loveliness. It was as if a spell of softness was being cast over him.

A spell that felt like bolls of cotton imbued with the fragrance of a French perfume. And as quickly as the spell had come, it was broken by a voice from inside the carriage.

"What you boys doin' out here in the middle of nowhere?"

The raspy voice belonged to Jemmy Jem, the young woman's Black nanny, who emerged from the cart as she spoke. "Ain't nothin' out here but varmints and Johnny Reb." Then she laughed a big, sincere, jolly laugh. "And you white boys shore don't look like none 'a those." She was a large-boned woman of maturity, with a grace and dignity of her own. She strode up to Boone and surveyed him from the top of his head to the leather of his boots. "You ain't from these parts, is you?" Jemmy said.

The young angel stepped back from Boone, releasing him from her eyes, and Boone found his voice. "No ma'am, we ain't," he said to Jemmy Jem.

"Well, what you doin' here then?" the nanny asked.

Boone cleared his throat, as if speaking, even thinking, had become difficult for him. "I'm takin' my wares to Chattanooga. I'm gonna sell them there."

"What kind o' wares?" Jemmy asked.

The angel glided away from them, back to the carriage. Boone could not take his eyes from her.

"Her name is Mardi," Jemmy said as she saw Boone's eyes follow her mistress. "Mardi Jamerson. She's the last of the line." Jemmy Jem sighed deeply from a remembered tragedy. "A line of greatness and distinction."

Mardi effortlessly entered the lacquered coach and settled back into the leather seat. Her curiosity sated, she stared straight ahead, as if Boone and Jebber had not even existed.

Boone's eyes couldn't leave her, though he was still powerless to utter a word. Then Jemmy Jem poked him. "What kind o' wares, I said?"

"Uhh...pottery," Boone stammered. "Yellow ware."

Jemmy Jem laughed her joyous laugh. "Why Mardi loves yellow ware. But only if it's unique. And only if it's delicate."

"I do it myself," Boone said. "Ain't like none other."

Jemmy smiled. "But is it delicate?"

Boone lowered his head, almost embarrassed. "I think it's good work. It's fine...and it's good."

Jebber came up for air. "You only have to see it, ma'am. Boone's

the best. We got a cartload on the boat down there and we's takin'
it to big city. Do you know which way *is* big city, ma'am?"

Jemmy touched Jebber's cheek with a soft and loving hand.
"Why yer just a child, ain't you?" she said, smiling sweetly to
him.

"He's strong as an ox," Boone said. "He's my brother-in-law,
but he's a touch slow."

Jemmy smiled knowingly at Boone. "I'll bet he keeps yer sister
happy."

Jebber blushed. "That he does," Boone said, chuckling. "That
he does."

Jemmy Jem turned back to the coach. "We just came from
the city. We was goin' somewheres else, but I think we got us a
good reason to go back there now." She called up to the driver.
"Reynard, turn about. Turn about at once and take the mistress
where she was."

Reynard hawed the black stallion. The ornate coach wheeled
to the left, inscribed a half-circle, and Jemmy Jem climbed in
beside her mistress. "I reckon we'll see you again," Jemmy said
to Boone. The coach sped away in another whirlwind of dust.

"I ain't never seen a woman what looks like that," Boone said
as the coach disappeared behind the murky swirl.

Inside the lushly upholstered carriage Mardi turned to Jemmy
Jem, smiled, and nodded.

TWENTY-FIVE

Jebber had once again taken up his position between the cart shafts and was pulling Boone's precious cargo down the road. The road to big city. Boone walked lazily next to the cart, a long piece of sweet grass between his teeth.

"I wish we had us another mule," Jebber said. Beads of sweat glistened on his forehead in the heat of the afternoon.

"A horse would be even better," Boone replied. "That way I could ride it instead of walkin.'"

"Boone!" Jebber cried, "I wants a mule to pull this here cart."

Boone laughed. "Well, I want a horse to ride. Besides, that lil' ol' cart ain't nothin' to a big, strong fella' like you, is it?"

Jebber, loving any compliment or the slightest stroke of his fragile child's ego, puffed out his chest. "Heck no, it ain't. I kin handle way more than this."

"I know you can," Boone said, smiling. "But I do wish we had a horse."

"I wish we was *there*," Jebber said.

Then they were silent as the heat and humidity seemed to deny all thought. The earth, and all the growing things upon it, however, loved the moist warmth of that spring afternoon. The primeval forest had been called to life and was doing its work of living: sending sap and juices and energy up from deep roots into every stem, branch, leaf, and fiber. Growing upward toward the sun, expanding themselves into the light.

And from out of the silence, a picture of Mardi crept into Boone's mind. It was an image that became so luminous and real that Boone had to shake his head to convince himself that

87

she was not there with him.

Jebber, as if seeing the same image, said, "I hope we see that colored lady agin. I liked her. And that Mardi had the whitest skin what I ever did see." Jebber looked over at Boone. "You think we'll see them again, Boone?"

Boone blinked himself back from his trance. "I hope so," he softly said.

Then, from down the roadway, came the dull tramp of hooves, accompanied by the clank of gear and the chink of bridle straps and stirrups. Four horsemen appeared in the distance, riding at a gallop.

Jebber and Boone turned to look. "Great God almighty!" Boone said.

Jebber exclaimed. "We got horses comin' fer us. They's gonna take us to town, Boone." Jebber took off his cavalry hat and waved it over his head. "Ain't this our lucky day?"

Boone saw something different in the onrushing riders. "I don't think luck's got no place in this, Jebber."

The horsemen came upon them, reined in their mounts, and fanned out, slowly circling Jebber and Boone. They were a ragtag bunch on unmatched horses. One man had nothing but a blanket for a saddle. Another had fashioned his bridle out of stripped and braided tree bark. Their uniforms were filthy and thin with wear. They were Confederate riders.

Jebber was ecstatic. "Hidee! Y'all just ride out fer us? Well, here we is!"

The lead man moved his pale horse in front of Jebber. A brace of pistols was slung butt-to-butt on his belt. His hands moved with the speed of a striking rattler as he cross-drew his guns and leveled a bore at each of Jebber's eyes.

"Shut up, ya miserable blue-belly bastard!" he roared.

Jebber, more hurt and confused than scared, turned to Boone. "Boone, why?" And he pulled up his shirt and looked at his belly. "Why'd he call me that?"

"Don't do nothin' crazy," Boone whispered to Jebber. "They's serious."

Another rider, on a chestnut-red horse, sauntered alongside Jebber, drew his sword, speared Jebber's hat, and snatched it off his head. Jebber swiped at his precious plumage but his hand came up empty. "Mister, gimme back my hat!" he shouted.

The rider laughed belligerently and raised the hat high overhead on his sword, taunting Jebber. In response, Jebber pulled a cross-draw of his own; a short machete he carried for cutting through the forest was up thrust in one hand, and the glistening Yankee saber held firm in the other. "Mister," he said, "don't get me riled! I ain't a body to be trifled with."

"Jebber, stop!" Boone cried.

Behind Jebber, a young horseman eased himself down from his black steed and slid a rifle out of his scabbard. He slammed the hardwood stock of the weapon high into the crown of Jebber's head. A deep, crimson gash split Jebber's scalp and a stream of blood began to streak his face. Jebber didn't even blink. He dropped his machete, wiped the wound, and stared disbelievingly at the blood on his hand. "That's my blood," he said. "Doggonit. Now ya done made me mad!"

Jebber threw down the saber in disgust. He whirled around to face his assailant, meaty fists clenched knuckle-white. The youthful rider pointed the rifle at Jebber. "Stay back from me," he said. Jebber's right hand shot out and knocked the rifle from the ragged soldier's hand before the boy could even think of taking a shot.

Boone rushed to Jebber and wrapped him up in a bear hug. Jebber tried to shake him off like a bronco trying to shuck a rodeo rider. But somehow, Boone held tight. "Jebber, please… Jebber! I'm beggin' you. Be nice to the boy. It's just a little misunderstandin'."

Two loud shots rang out. Boone put his hands over his ears. "Jebber," Boone shouted in a kind of panic. "They gonna shoot us. We don't wanna die here, not like this."

And hearing that, Jebber came to his senses. Cool as ice, he turned to the man on the pale horse, where curls of powder smoke rose from his pistols. "Mister," Jebber said, "I'll forgive that boy for what he done to me. But if you hurt Boone, I swear, I'll kill you graveyard dead. It's my job to protect him."

Then a man astride a white horse cantered into the trouble. His only weapon was a bow and a quiver of arrows slung over his shoulder. He spoke with authority. "You men are prisoners of the Confederate States Army. You will soon appear before my commander, General Nathan Bedford Forrest, to face charges of servin', abettin', and spyin' for the Union forces of the North."

Boone was shocked. "Spyin'? We's just takin' my wares to Chattanooga."

"That proves yer lyin'," the bowman said. "Y'all are headed south and Chattanooga's back up north."

"You mean we missed it?" Boone asked.

"You spies can't fool me. You know damn sure where y'all are."

"How could we spy? We didn't even know there was a war on."

The soldiers laughed at the absurdity of Boone's claim. The man with Jebber's hat atop his sword burst in, "Then how y'explain this here Yankee colonel's cutter?" The boy soldier picked up Jebber's saber and looked closely at the blade. "An' this here etchin' on the sword," he called out. "Colonel Daniel Hennesey. Scourge of the South."

Boone pleaded with them. "Gentlemen, I vouch my word. We came upon these in a coffin."

The man with the pistols spat upon the ground. "If you's spies, y'all be shot at dawn. If it's grave robbin' ya done, well, then, you reckons to have your necks stretched in the public square. Which do ya favor?"

Boone took a hard look at the ragged men circled around him. He knew there was nothing further to be said to the hollow-eyed Rebels. He sucked his cheeks and spat in the dust of the roadway. "Come to that, I ain't choicey."

TWENTY-SIX

Boone and Jebber both hauled the cart down the road as the four horsemen rode beside them, atop their mounts with weapons drawn. They traveled the La Fayette Road and Boone began to have a precognition in the heat and dust. He began to see things that weren't there, but would be on September 19 and 20 in the year of our Lord of 1863. In the haze of the afternoon, Boone saw the road lined by ricks of gray- and blue-clad corpses stacked like split cordwood. Mutilated bodies of young Yankees and Rebels who had slaughtered one another in the killing that would come to be known as the Battle of Chickamauga. He saw dead mules and horses rotting in the sun. And the twisted metal and scorched, smoldering wood of rigs and weapons. Boone saw war, and he saw Hell. He could not stomach the horror of his vision and he rubbed his eyes and shook his head violently to clear the apparition from his sight.

Jebber saw Boone's strange actions. "What's wrong with you, Boone?"

Boone stammered. "I…I just need some water."

Jebber, unafraid, called to his captors. "Hey! Boone needs somethin' to drink. Y'all give him some water."

The four horsemen found the demand hilarious. They laughed and guffawed with animal-like glee. The rider with the bow and arrow sniggered at Jebber. "He don't get nothin' till General Forrest sees 'im. Then he's gonna get dead!" They all laughed again.

Boone and Jebber trudged on through the heat, silent and fearful. At last, the captors and their prisoners came to Lee and Gordon's Mill, a whitewashed clapboard A-frame perched high beside West Chickamauga Creek. A small detachment of Confederate guards was positioned about the entrance to the mill house. The horseman with the brace of pistols swung down off his pale mount and spoke briefly to one of the guards. The guard looked over at Boone and Jebber, shook his head in disgust, and spat on the ground. Then he knocked on the slab wood door, pushed it open, and barked his report. His voice echoed through the hollow mill.

"General Forrest, sir. Spies!"

The guard then snapped to attention beside the door. Brigadier General Nathan Bedford Forrest emerged from the dank gloom of the mill into the heat and light of the sweltering haze. He was a spare man, chisel-cheeked and with a goatee that lent him a Mephistophelian air. And following in his wake came a coterie of aides and adjutants. They were foppish, white-gloved majors and courtly colonels. The aristocracy of the South. Dressed for the theater, the play of war. They were perfumed, trimmed, and coiffed; their uniforms crisp and polished and bespangled with campaign ribbons. One held a delicate lavender-scented handkerchief to his nose. Another absent-mindedly twirled the tips of his waxed moustache. A third carried with great affection an ivory cane, capped by a carved head of an African chieftain.

General Forrest and his gaggle of dandies crossed the mill yard until the general stood before Jebber and Boone. His merciless eyes studied them from head to toe, as if inspecting fresh hands for his notorious "nigger yard" in Memphis. Then he pronounced his judgment.

"Hang 'em," he snapped, in a voice that sounded like the hiss of a snake. He turned brusquely away and moved toward his silky-white steed held at the ready by a coal-black groom in red foxhunt livery. Soldiers quickly wrapped hemp cord around the wrists of Boone and Jebber.

Boone yelled at Forrest. "Hey, mister! Now just a God blame minute!"

Wham! A rifle butt slammed into Boone's gut. "Shut up, ya damn spy," the snarling Rebel guard sputtered. Boone dropped to the ground, gasping for air and retching.

Jebber squeezed his eyes shut tight, raised his bound wrists—straining muscles bulging—and snapped the braided hemp as if it were nothing more than cotton lisle.

The snarling Rebel kicked Boone, spitting his words at him. "That ain't no mister. That's General Nathan Bedford…" And that was as far as he got. For as he raised his boot to kick Boone again, Jebber's meaty hands snatched onto his leg. He lifted the soldier clear off the ground and torqued the limb until it snapped like a wishbone. Then he dropped the screaming Rebel to the ground where he lay writhing in the dust of the mill yard beside Boone.

Another soldier charged Jebber with a fixed bayonet. Jebber, with the moves of a matador, sidestepped the charge, grabbed the passing rifle barrel and began to spin in circles like a discus hurler. Then he flung the soldier—rifle and all—through the air, like a sack of corn.

From all sides, guns were raised up to the ready, and hammers cocked. "Hold your fire!" General Forrest shouted.

Jebber bent over Boone. He tenderly propped his brother-in-law up on one knee. The general moved away from his horse and stood over them.

"Who the devil are you?" he said with not a little amazement in his voice.

Boone spat blood into the dust. "We ain't no spies, sir."

"Where you two from?" the general asked.

"Coker Creek Hollow," Jebber answered.

"Where in hell is that?"

Boone, still hunched over, raised his head and saw rifles pointed at him and Jebber. "I'd offer it's closer to Heaven than it is to Hell. Leastwise what you got around here." Then he remembered his vision of the dead. "And what yer gonna have here in time to come."

That caught the general's ear. "What's that supposed to mean? What do you know?"

Boone staggered to his feet. "Sometimes I can see things, sir. Don't necessarily mean they're true." His knees buckled and Jebber caught his arm to hold him up. "I seen death here, sir. Along the roadside, bodies stacked like cordwood. Gray and blue." Boone looked the general straight in the eyes. "Death don't care what color the uniforms are."

General Forrest saw that Boone had a depth to him that he did not quite understand. He almost felt a sympathy for this backwoods farmer. A sympathy he hadn't felt since the War Between the States began. "You speak the truth there, son." Forrest scanned the ranks and his eyes fell upon the horseman brandishing the bow and arrows atop his black mount. "Where'd you come by these two?"

"Sir, it was yon crick a ways."

Forrest's gaze followed the ribbon of water that snaked past the mill, its curves undulating like a copperhead. "Chickamauga," he breathed aloud into the air, "Cherokees named it. This crick and the river it flows from." He turned back to Boone. "In their tongue, it means River of Death."

Boone nodded. "Then maybe they saw what I saw."

The general looked into Boone's eyes. "I had a dream the other night that the river ran red with blood."

"I seen what caused the blood, sir. I seen the piles of soldiers," Boone said.

For an instant, compassion flashed in General Forrest's eyes. "Oh, my Lord," he said, envisioning the horror to come.

The black-mounted horseman came forward with Jebber's sword in hand. "General, when we rode upon 'em, the big one, he had this."

General Forrest took the sword and read the inscription. "Hennesey?" He turned to Boone. "You know who this man is?"

"One of them wearin' the blue coats, sir," Boone replied.

"That's correct, son," the general said. "But a Yankee officer. A colonel. What they call a 'Northern Gentleman.' He ordered his men to set upon every Southern gal as if she were a common whore."

Boone spat blood into the dust. "I don't reckon that much concerns us, sir."

"Why's that? You have no womenfolk to call your own?"

"We got women, sir. But we ain't got no part in this fight of yours."

The general pointed the sword at the broken-legged soldier. "Seems you do now."

Jebber hung his head.

"How'd you get this sword?" Forrest asked.

"Wasn't Boone's fault," Jebber said. "It was me. I done took it."

"You hush up, Jebber. I'll take care of things now," Boone said. Then he turned to the general. "There was five of 'em, sir. I reckon now they had nary shot nor powder. I didn't know that then. And Jebber here, he don't care about such things. They came at us with their guns and swords and bayonets flashin'. Jebber had nothin' but his hands, yet you seen yourself what he can do."

Boone pointed to the sword in the general's grasp. "The one who held that, well, Jebber fixed his neck like he just done to that boy's leg."

Jebber was completely buffaloed. Not sure who he was supposed to have killed and who he was not. But he knew Boone was not telling the truth. "Boone, why are you tellin' this man these things?"

General Forrest bore in on Jebber. "Did you kill Colonel Hennesey?"

Jebber, flustered to the bone, could only stutter.

Boone came to his rescue, slipping between the two men. "Yes, sir, he did. By God and on the lives of my loved ones, he did."

General Forrest stepped back and raised the sword. "By proclamation of our president, Jefferson Davis, a bounty has been placed upon the head of that damn Hennesey."

He brought the sword down out of the air and Jebber ducked, fearing the loss of *his* head. Instead, General Forrest presented the gleaming saber to Jebber. "May I bestow this treasure of the battlefield to its rightful owner."

With wide eyes and open mouth, Jebber accepted the sword. Forrest continued: "Sir, I, indeed, *all* of General Lee's army and the besieged citizens under our protection, are sorely in your debt." Then he snapped his fingers and one of his foppish aides, complete with plumed hat, stepped forward. The general motioned to a briefcase the aide had chained to his wrist. "Open it," he said.

The dandy unlocked the case and General Forrest thrust his hand into it. He rummaged about and came forth with a fistful of Confederate scrip. "Name your price," he said to Jebber.

The overgrown man-boy was dizzy with glee. Never before had anyone offered him anything of the slightest worth. Never before had anyone called him "sir." Boone lit up in a toothy grin. "Don't be shy, now, Jebber. You're a hero. You've earned what all y'ask for."

Jebber grinned at Boone. "Thankee," he said. Then he pointed to the aide's plumed slouch hat. "I wants a hat with a big feather like this feller's here. An' I want a horse an' guns an' a dandified gittup like y'all wear, so's I kin ride with you boys."

General Forrest's grim face cracked into a tight-lipped smile. "You'll have everything you ask for, son," and he thrust the wad of money into Jebber's pocket.

Boone could only stand there, scratching his head in disbelief, as Jebber giggled with delight, like the child he was.

TWENTY-SEVEN

On the outskirts of the town of La Fayette, Georgia, it was a quiet night. Mounted sentries lurked beneath the shadowy boughs of flowering peach trees, keeping a lookout for any Yankee incursion. Fireflies glided through the dark air like slow-moving stars. The mosquitoes had not yet come to life for it was a bit too early in the year, and the nightingales trilled graceful songs into the soft, Georgia night.

The town itself had curled up in slumber. The streets and storefronts were dark and empty. All was peaceful and tranquil, except for the Red Rabbit Inn.

Rouge light and pianola music and raucous laughter spilled from inside this honky-tonk saloon and hotbed hotel. Two Rebel pickets were posted out front at the door. The sweaty interior was filled with a blue blanket of plantation tobacco and greasy smoke from flickering gas lamps. Through the haze and din, circles of soldiers were cast about the room, reeling around bawdyhouse gals flashing billowy folds of petticoats. The soldiers laughed and shouted to each other as they pinched and prodded the ladies of the night, and the gals squealed and giggled with each pinch, anticipating a fine payday at the end of their long night.

Over the noise, a baritone standing at the bar with a tankard of ale in hand bellowed out "Morgan's War Song," the battle hymn of Kentucky's famed cavalry:

"Ye sons of the South
take your weapons in hand,
For the foot of the foe
hath insulted your land.

Sound! Sound the loud alarm!
Arise! Arise and arm!
Let the hand of each freeman
grasp the sword to maintain
Those rights which, once lost,
we can never regain."

On top of the bar, a huge pair of boots, freshly blacked and shined, pounded the mahogany in step to the tune. A giant, resplendent in swanky, dove-gray cavalryman's cloth, brass buttons, whorls of gold braid, and plumed slouch hat, danced furiously. A simple man-child transformed—it was Jebber. A gal was hooked on each of his arms, all bosom, legs, and lace, high-kicking their heels and flashing bare, pantyless glimpses beneath their wide-hooped skirts. A band of soldiers was pressed tight to the bar, thoroughly enjoying the view. The gathered men broke into the chorus of the song:

"Gather fast 'neath our flag,
for 'tis God's own decree
That its folds shall still float
o'er a land that is free."

With one arm, Jebber lifted a gal clear off her feet as his other hand thrust his saber high into the blue smoke. The men erupted in Rebel yells and whoops of triumph, and a great exhilaration filled the hall.

Boone sat at a table with General Forrest and his staff. With their feathered caps, curled locks, and haughty airs, Forrest's aides looked more like French kings than Rebel soldiers. It seemed the only fighting they did was with words.

"It is a question of the Constitution," one of the dandies said with firm resolve. "Our government, any damn government, draws its power from the consent of those governed." The colonel pounded the table with his fist. "And we do not consent!"

A major took up the argument, for men of war seem always to need a rationalization for killing. "Constitution, State's Rights, call it by the words you will. Above all, it's simple liberty. Our inalienable right to choose the path of our lives, and to provide for our children and our children's children by the means which we know." The major was oblivious to the din of the hall, for he had become hypnotized by his own oratory. "We must remain unhindered in our pursuits by the tyranny and oppression of a foreign gov'ment in the North. For we are men—free men—of action and deed who follow our own destiny under the guidance of God's divine hand."

The colonel raised his glass in salute. "Here, here. Well said, Major." And the gathered dandies raised their drinks in toast to the eloquent justification for the slaughter that was taking place all about them in the United States of America in the year of our Lord of 1863.

Boone, emboldened by drink, could not resist joining in. "Now just a henpeckin' second. Those are might fine words, but a man told me y'all was fightin' because the coloreds want to be free."

His remark was met by blank stares, then in the next moment, hearty laughter. "If only it were so simple," another major said. "If only the matter of our secession was merely as trivial as that."

General Forrest had heard enough of this pansy patter. "The hell it ain't! War means fightin' and fightin' means killin'. And if all that blood that's been spilled, and all those lives that we've takin' from the earth ain't to keep hold of our slaves, then what in damnation is it for?"

With that, Forrest rose from his seat, swept his hat off the table, and tucked it under one arm. He lifted his glass of cane-reed whisky and tossed it back. Without another word, he pushed through the raucous crowd, heading for the door.

His adjutants promptly collected their white gloves and polished sabers and plumed hats and toadied quickly after their departing general.

Boone was left alone at the table with a half-dozen empty tumblers of whisky, an empty bottle, and one still half-full. Jebber approached the table with his two gals clinging to his arms. "Hey ye, Boone." Then he noticed all the whisky. "I see you got yerself a powerful thirst."

Boone knocked back a shot and then clapped the glass down on the table. "Yep, might say I do, Jebber." He gave the gaudily made-up working girls a scornful once over. "But no more than yours, I'd say."

The girls giggled as Jebber squeezed them to his sides. "Ya know, 'long with this dandy coat and drawers and shiny boots that nice general gave me, he done stuffed my pockets with what they call Confederate dollars. He said it ain't worth much, but I tell ya, Boone, these here fine gals offered up to see I spend it right. Lord knows how we was so lucky to find such a friendly place to come to." He squeezed the girls once more, and they squealed again. "But find it we shore did. How'd we do that, Boone?"

Boone threw down another gill of hooch. "Born under a lucky star, I reckon." He pushed the bottle to the center of the table and pulled out the chair next to him. "Take a load off, Jebber, and wet yer whistle."

"Thankee, Boone," Jebber said grinning like the fool he was. "But these here ladies went and got me a dee-luxe room upstairs so's I could go off to war on a good night's sleep."

"Well, dang!" Boone sarcastically said. "This shore is the most *friendly* town in the whole damn world. And I'll bet that good night's sleep won't come afore some serious stump jumpin', eh Jebber?

The dandified ox pulled loose from the ladies clutches and bent down to whisper excitedly in Boone's ear. "They even promised to help me wash up in hot bathwater," Jebber said.

Boone had heard enough. He rose to his feet and said, "Jebber, you got any of that money left?"

"Sure do," Jebber said. He plucked the scrip from his pocket and held it out to Boone. "Take as much as you want."

Boone snatched the whole wad out of Jebber's hand and stuffed it down the bodice of the gal nearest him. "Here. You gals done cleaned him up already. Now git!"

TWENTY-EIGHT

It was 4:00 AM, the gas lamps had all been extinguished, but Jebber was wide-awake. Still wearing his uniform and boots, he sat on the edge of the bed in the dee-luxe room of the Red Rabbit Inn. He swung his legs like a little boy, giddy with anticipation of the day to come. "We're headin' out at dawn, Boone."

Boone stood at the window, gazing out, a dark shadow in the pale shine of the moon. "Jebber, I thought about it and then I thought some more." The shadow figure turned to face Jebber, who could see no detail. Only an ominous silhouette spoke to him. "I just cannot let you run off to fight in some war."

Jebber would have none of it. "You best stop that thinkin', Boone, for you can't stop me. I'm goin' and that's all there is to it."

The shadow spoke again. "You don't even know what it is yer fightin' for."

Jebber took affront. "Sure I do. I'm fightin' to keep our slaves."

Boone's patience was worn thin. "We don't have no slaves, you fool! Do you see any coloreds here? Did we ever have any coloreds at the farm? Wake up, Jebber. It's just you and me what's here."

"Well, Boone," Jebber said, "thing of it is, by the time I git back, we'll have more slaves than you can shake a stick at."

The shadow turned back to the moonlight. "You have no goddamn idea what all yer gettin' into."

"Oh yes I do," Jebber said. "I surely do. I am ridin' into battle to kill all them miserable blue-belly Yankee bastards. Sir!"

The shadow cocked his head. "Sir?"

"Yep. That's what ya say when yer in the army. Y'always say

'sir.' I like that about the army. It's most polite."

"I don't give a fat pig's ass what they been tellin' you, Jebber. Nor what you been tellin' me. You ain't *goin'!* And the reason you ain't goin' is 'cause of Jewel."

At the sound of his wife's name, Jebber stopped his kicking and rose to his feet. "What you bring her up for?"

"Because before we left, I made her a promise. I swore I'd bring you back with me, safe as the day you was born."

Jebber began to pace the room. Boone had hit a nerve. "Don't you drag Jewel into this. I refuse to talk 'bout Jewel an' any 'a this. You just could never understand."

"Jebber, I can't believe this. Are you sayin', this is all 'cause of Jewel?"

Jebber hung his head like a scolded little boy.

" 'Cause 'a Jewel?" Boone continued. "Nobody 'round here even knows Jewel's name. The Rebs don't know her. The Yankees don't know her. And for damn sure the coloreds don't know her neither."

"Boone, it ain't fer *them*. It's fer *her*. I know plain as day what she thinks 'a me."

"Jebber, Jewel loves you. She loves you more than a bitch hound loves her first batch 'a pups."

Jebber continued to pace, his shiny new boots snapping against the oak floor. "I don't doubt that. She's sweet with her words, an' she always tends to my needs real good. Come night, when she takes to ridin' my big bull, why she wiggles an' screams loud as a stuck sow. I know she likes that. An' I'm grateful to God in His Highest that she's always rarin' to go. Again and again."

The shadow in the moonlight laughed heartily and Jebber started to giggle in turn. But then his tone turned somber. "Yet all that don't make amends for the way I feel when I look into her eyes. 'Cause Boone, don't matter how long or hard I peer, I just never don't find that look 'a respect. I know Jewel loves me. But she loves me like a boy. An' I want to be her man. That's why I'm goin' off to fight in this war. So's I can come home a hero."

"But Jebber, you already are a hero. Ask anyone in this whole army of the South. They all know you're a hero. You just need to tell Jewel what you done."

Jebber looked hard at the shadow, but Boone had stepped back into the curtain's clutch of darkness and was nothing but a dim outline in the thin wash of the moon. Almost as if he wasn't there. As if the real Boone had faded into a gray, amorphous shape. Jebber couldn't see Boone's eyes, and that worried him. He felt a change had come over his brother-in-law.

"Boone," Jebber said with anger in his voice, "you lied to that man today. I never stole that sword in no fight. An' I never did hear you tell no lie before. An' it hurt. Hurt somethin' bad. But then I thought an' I thought real hard, an' I come to hope you only done that so's to keep us from gettin' killed."

The shadow turned back to the window, looking into the moonlight, and sighed deeply. "That's all I could do. I couldn't do no more than lie. I was lookin' out for you, Jebber. The same way I can trust on you watchin' out for me."

"Well, that may be," Jebber said to the back of the shadow. "But if I was to go home an' say to Jewel what you told the general today, I do not believe I could find one lonesome reason in this whole world for wantin' to live another day."

And with that, Jebber snatched up his plumed hat and his spoils-of-war saber, crossed the room, and walked out the door.

In the pale gloss of the moon, the shadow that was Boone watched Jebber step off the boardwalk to the hitching post down below. He untethered the reins of a fine white horse, slipped a foot in the stirrup, and swung up astride his mount. In the milky light, the road looked white as salt, and Jebber riding off, high in the saddle, looked every inch a soldier.

TWENTY-NINE

In the town square of La Fayette, Boone began to unload his pottery from the cart, which was now drawn by a mule. He placed a few of Delilah's quilts on the grass beneath the great spreading limbs of an ancient black oak tree. The Spanish moss that hung down from the branches lent the tree an otherworldly look. But the dappled shade was welcome relief from the unseasonable heat, which hung on longer than Boone could ever remember a spring heatwave lasting. The ridge of high pressure that had descended on the tail of the snake moon, stifling the region from west of the Appalachians to the eastern seaboard, had not abated. And the dryness and energy of the high-pressure ions made everything strangely edgy, with the vaguest feeling in the atmosphere of some impending doom.

Boone, carefully and lovingly, brushed straw off each piece of his art and set them down on the quilts like toy soldiers in battle formation. There were rows of plates and pitchers, bowls and jugs, cups and saucers, vases and boxes. And their soft, lustrous patina gave off a glow in the shaded light of almost unearthly beauty. He was proud of his creations and was eager for the town folk of La Fayette to appreciate and, hopefully, purchase them.

As the noon hour neared, a small crowd of citizens began to gather in front of Boone's display. There was much touching of the pieces and many *oohs* and *aahs* over their fine craftsmanship. However, only a few sales were made. Boone had set prices high, not unfairly so he thought, but high enough to keep the *hoi polloi* from making any foolish and impulsive purchases of his wares. He wanted gentlemen and fine ladies to be the owners of his art. And he wanted the gentry to know his name. He wanted them to know that Boone Dillard was the creator of the pieces they had purchased. And in the shifting light cast through the shadowy Spanish moss, Boone began to fall into a reverie. He slipped into a daydream of desire and envisioned himself a gentleman of substance, promenading the streets of a big city, greeted by the locals with a "Good day, Boone" and a "Hidee, Mister Dillard" and a whispered "There goes Boone Dillard." And he felt very happy with himself.

Then he saw it. Turning a corner and heading for the town square was the white, lacquered carriage with the gold filigree trim. Atop the coach in his black livery, Reynard paced the black stallion at a leisurely canter. It trundled straight up to the town square and stopped. The carriage door opened and out came Jemmy Jem. She turned back and extended her hand inside, and Mardi, taking the hand for support, emerged from the coach. She wore a flowing white dress and stepped to the street beneath the shadow of a parasol, and she was an ethereal vision.

Boone saw her and his pulse quickened. The blood began to race through his veins, carrying excitement and anticipation to every part of his body. He was beginning to perspire, for her beauty was overwhelming to him.

With Jemmy Jem in the lead, Mardi glided effortlessly to Boone's display. The town folk gathered about the quilts instinctively parted before her, giving Mardi an unencumbered view of Boone's pottery. Her head was cast down beneath the parasol as she came forward, and Boone could not quite see her face. It was as if Mardi were teasing him, holding back her beauty from his gaze. Holding back from Boone's eyes the lustrous whiteness of her skin.

Mardi looked across the rows of Boone's art and he could smell the faintest hint of lilacs surrounding her. She bent down and touched a few of the pieces, running her fingers over the curves of a vase and tracing the floral design of a pitcher. Then she picked up a small box and gave out a soft laugh as she opened it. An inscription inside the lid read: "For My Secrets." The thought tickled Mardi, and a sound like the trill of songbirds escaped from her mouth. She tilted back the parasol and finally revealed her face. "I have many secrets," she said as she looked into Boone's eyes. "Don't you, Mister...?"

Boone's breath was taken away as her eyes penetrated into his depths. Those impossibly blue eyes caused an electricity to shoot through him, sweeping over his consciousness and entangling his will. His voice caught in his throat, but he managed to say, "Dillard, ma'am. Boone Dillard."

Mardi's lips parted and she smiled at Boone. "Your work is beautiful, Mister Dillard. So elegant and understanding of the mysteries of nature." She extended the secrets box to Boone. "I'll take this one."

Boone held out his hand, Mardi placed the box on his palm, and their flesh met for the first time. A blue spark leapt at the contact and Boone quickly drew back his hand, shocked by the elemental charge.

Mardi laughed again, her songbirds flitting into the air. "My goodness, Mister Dillard. It seems we have a spark between us. I wonder just what that might mean?" She lowered her eyes demurely, as if suddenly shamed by the suggestion.

"I don't rightly know, ma'am," Boone stammered.

"Please, call me Mardi," and she extended her hand to Boone. But Boone didn't take it, he had been rendered immobile by the spark, her eyes, and her beauty.

"You can take my hand, Mister Dillard. I promise, I won't bite you," Mardi said with a flash of charm and light in her eyes as she looked coyly at Boone.

Boone came out of his trance and took her hand. "I'm pleased to make your acquaintance, Mardi. Please, call me Boone."

She smiled. "Well, I shall…Boone."

He had never heard his name uttered by a person of such grace, such breeding. His heart leapt in his chest. His daydream was beginning to turn itself into reality.

In a swirl of white taffeta, Mardi moved her hand over Boone's pieces, saying, "I'll take this one, and this, and these…and this one, too." Then she came across a vase decorated with blades of grass and the scant outline of a dragonfly set to alight upon one of the blades. "Oh, I just love this. It is so sensitive, so in touch with the fleeting truth at the heart of existence." She looked up again, into Boone's eyes. "You know things, don't you, Boone."

As their eyes joined, Boone felt their energies merge. Her eyes drew his essence into hers and he relinquished all control to her power. In that instant, he gave himself over to the rapturous feeling that was swirling its vortex through him. Her eyes were turning him into the liquid gold that he used to enhance the life force of his plowed field. Everything in him was turning in on itself as Boone allowed his thoughts to be swept up by the whirlwind of emotion that was racing through him.

Mardi spoke again. "You understand more than you're willing to admit."

"I s'pose I know some about life, ma'am," Boone finally said.

"I would say you know about life, and the things *beyond* life," Mardi said. "Why, it wouldn't surprise me at all, Boone, if you were one of those rare people who understand how easy it is to slip back and forth between this world and the other." She smiled her radiance again. "It's all existence. It's really all the same. And we both know that, don't we, Boone."

Then she rose up, turned in a swirl of whiteness, twirled her parasol, and glided off in her effortless, elegant manner, off to her white, lacquered coach. Jemmy Jem laughed her warm chortle. "I believe the mistress has taken a fancy to you, son. I'll pay you for the pieces Miss Mardi has chosen." Jemmy looked across the pottery on Delilah's quilts. "You do fine work, son. Most sensitive. But truth be told, I'm hankerin' after these two quilts y'all got yer wares set upon."

"They're not mine." said Boone. "My grandmother made them."

"Well, I see where you got yer talent," Jemmy said. "They say it runs in the blood. And they also say it often skips a generation. If you don't mind my askin', do yer mama or yer daddy have any abilities like y'all and yer gramma?"

Boone shook his head. "They're both dead."

"Oh, I'm sorry, son. What happened?"

"Cholera got 'em," Boone said softly.

"Well, all things live and all things die," Jemmy said comfortingly. "I'm sure they was fine people and you was most lucky to be born of them."

"Thank you," Boone said. "I reckon I was."

Jemmy Jem laughed and Boone felt reassuring warmth coming from her inner joy. "And this is yo' lucky day. Miss Mardi will take what she picked out and I will take those two lovely quilts." She looked across Boone's art one more time. "And unless I miss my guess, I do believe our household could use *all* yer wares."

Boone couldn't believe what he had just heard. "You want to

buy everything I have?"

Jemmy Jem swept her arm over the two quilts. "The whole lot, Mister Boone Dillard. The whole lot!"

She turned back to the coach and called out, "Reynard! You come down here and help Mister Dillard pack these precious things back on his cart. Then have him follow us home." She turned to Boone. "Thank you, sir. Thank you for bein' alive." And as she walked back to the white, lacquered coach, Boone could see Mardi sitting inside, gazing out the window and smiling at him. It seemed to Boone the smile of angels.

THIRTY

The black stallion clip-clopped impatiently as it drew Mardi's carriage through a tunneled canopy of ancient oaks dangling tangles of the ubiquitous Spanish moss. Boone's mule-drawn cart, piled again with his wares, followed closely behind, or as closely as it could, for the stallion rebelled at moving at the slow pace of a mere draught animal. And now Reynard could barely hold back the black beast as it saw home and anticipated its dinner of sweet mash in the stables.

The little procession emerged from the green passageway onto the cobbled stone driveway of a magnificent plantation house, complete with columned entranceway. It was clean and white and Boone had never seen anything so grand.

Reynard brought the carriage to a stop and clambered down to open the coach door. Mardi and Jemmy Jem stepped out, giggling to each other like schoolgirls. They raced up the wide front steps and onto the shaded veranda. Jemmy Jem threw open the great front doors and Mardi rushed into her sanctuary.

Boone pulled in behind the white, lacquered carriage. "Welcome to Meadow Wood, Mister Boone," Reynard called out. "This here is Miss Mardi's home." Boone climbed down from his cart and stood before the broad stairway in awe. "Y'all go on in, Mister Boone. I'll see that your beautiful things get back to the pantry. And I'll handle them all most delicately, sir. Don't you mind."

But Boone could not respond. He stood fast, overwhelmed by the palatial estate. Never before had he imagined such grand splendor could find a place on this earth. And never before had he imagined that he would be invited to enter it.

Jemmy Jem appeared in the open doorway. She smiled and waved to Boone. "Y'all come on in, Mister Dillard. No sense standin' down there lookin'. Come on in and partake of our hospitality. Miss Mardi's waitin' for you."

THIRTY-ONE

As the sun began to set over Meadow Wood, Boone sat in the library, surrounded by leather, wood paneling, and finely bound books. He was clean-shaven, bathed, and dressed in crisp linen that Reynard told him had belonged to one of Mardi's brothers. They fit him beautifully and he looked most handsome. Almost as if he were born to such an elegant setting. He sat in a winged reading chair, gazing at the rows of books and sipping a glass of smooth Kentucky whisky, aged twenty years. And the glass contained ice, just as Jebber had once asked about. The ice cooled the whisky and Boone sipped slowly as the waning sun brushed the paneled room with its golden, twilight glow. And Boone felt very good with himself. He felt that his long voyage with his pottery had been well worth the effort. And he thought that if Jebber was going to go off and make a fool of himself, well, so be it. Boone had tried his best to stop him, but there was no talking sense into that big ox.

Boone sipped at his iced whisky and that was as far back as his thoughts would go. He was in the present, living in the now, and it felt good to him. Time didn't seem to matter at Meadow Wood. There seemed to be only the sensuality of the moment. Boone felt himself slipping out of the realm of memory and into the eternal present. He felt himself leaving the domain of obligations and responsibilities and entering a place of liberation. A place where *his* needs and *his* desires were all that was important. He sipped again at his whisky and he felt good, very good.

"Mister Dillard," Jemmy Jem said as she burst into the library, breaking Boone's reverie. Miss Mardi wanted me to pay you now for all yer fine things. I was jus' wonderin' what you thought might be a fair price."

"I don't rightly know," Boone said. "I ain't thought about what the lot is worth. I reckoned I'd sell 'em piece by piece."

Jemmy, ever the shrewd overseer of household business, said, "Well, I believe you should give me a better price for the whole lot than if you was to sell 'em one at a time. This way you done sold 'em all. An' you didn't have to waste none of yer precious time, neither." She looked out the window at the golden, fading light. "All our time on earth is precious, Mister Dillard. You're a man what knows that to be true, don't you, sir?"

"I do know that, Jemmy," Boone said. And he sipped leisurely at his Kentucky whisky, thoroughly enjoying the moment. "I'm sure whatever your mistress wants to pay me for my wares will be more than fair."

Jemmy clutched a fat leather purse in her hand. "Miss Mardi put these coins in this here poke an' didn't tell me how many to give you. I reckon you should just take 'em all." She emptied the purse onto Boone's lap—more gold coins than Boone had ever seen.

Boone grinned from ear to ear. "Why, thank you, Jemmy," he said as he dug his hand into the gleaming mound. The glow of the gold mesmerized Boone. He touched the pieces lovingly, then looked up at Jemmy Jem. "I ain't never had no real money before. I surely do like it."

Jemmy cackled her warm laugh. "Well, you deserve it, son. Yer hands have turned mere clay into something fine and beautiful, as if you done breathed the breath o' life into it. You have the power to do that, Boone. That dead ol' clay took on bodily form through yer hands. It took on the powerful mysteries of the spirit to become full with life." She put a warm and loving hand on Boone's shoulder. "A small pile of gold is just a triflin' reward for the magic you done made. The magic of life." And she kissed Boone softly on the cheek.

The golden glow in the room had faded into darkness. Jemmy Jem stepped back from Boone and then moved quickly about the library, lighting the gas lamps.

"Ain't this a fine room, Mister Dillard? The family spent many an evenin' in here, readin' and talkin'. An' Miss Mardi would play on that lil' harp-see-kord over there in the corner. She played it fine, too. But she don't play no more."

"Why not?" Boone asked as he began stuffing his pockets with the gold coins.

"She ain't of a mind to, now that the family's gone."

"Gone? What happened, Jemmy?"

"We don't need to talk 'bout that, Mister Dillard. Y'all is clean and bathed an' lookin' fine an' handsome in those clothes."

Boone chuckled, put the last coin in his tweed coat pocket, and finished his drink. "This has been a fine day for me, Jemmy. A day I'll always remember," he said through the glow of his whisky.

Jemmy Jem laughed her warmth into the room. "An' the night has jes' begun. Who knows *what* it has in store for you, Mister Boone Dillard." She walked to the intricately carved door of the library and swung it open. "Now, if you will follow me, sir, I will escort you to dinner. I know you must be just near starvin' to death."

Boone rose from his leather chair. "Why, yes, Jemmy, I am hungry." He stretched himself luxuriously. "Where's Miss Mardi?"

"She's in the dining room," Jemmy said. Then she smiled at Boone. "An' she's waitin' on you."

THIRTY-TWO

The dining room was a grand compliment to the splendor of the plantation house. Its walls were adorned with oil paintings of landscapes and hunting scenes, portraits and groupings of people who Boone guessed to be Mardi's family. Plush, velvety curtains hung ceiling to floor shrouding the windows, and a long, burnished maple table, complete with twelve richly upholstered chairs, stretched nearly the length of the spacious room. A row of five white candlesticks ran down the center of the table, but only one was lit. The candle, placed directly before Boone, flicked a wavy blue-and-yellow lick of flame.

Boone sat at the far end of the table. The place setting laid before him was of his own creation. In the soft glow of the candle, he lovingly touched his pieces of fired pottery, and he was proud of how easily they fit the elegant surroundings. The other end of the table was also set with a candlestick and his art, but the candle was not lit and Mardi was, in fact, not present.

Boone worried that she might not join him, that he wouldn't dine with her, and she would remain but a vision that had passed briefly into his life, never to be touched again.

The door creaked open. The room flushed with the brightness of the crystal chandelier that hung in the lofty entranceway outside the dining room. Boone's heart leapt with the flood of light as a silhouette sashayed into the room. But it was Jemmy Jem, her mittened hands holding a steaming soup tureen, which she placed atop a carved sideboard.

"Where's Mardi?" Boone called to Jemmy.

Jemmy uttered not a word. Instead, she placed an index finger to her lips to quiet Boone, almost as if speech were not allowed in such a polished and hallowed place. Reynard next entered the room carrying a platter of roast beef and garden vegetables. He set the platter next to the tureen and took up a position behind the chair at the head of the table.

And then, in the shimmering spill of the chandelier, as if walking on tendrils of light, Mardi appeared. An ethereal vision in white taffeta, seemingly beyond the touch of any man of this earth. Boone was awestruck, dazzled by her beauty in the crystalline rays of the chandelier. He tried to rise, but the strength of his limbs had been sapped, and he was slow and thick in his movements. By the time he was on his feet, Reynard had already pulled the chair back from the table, Mardi had glided to her seat, and the black tuxedoed manservant had deftly slid her into place. Boone now stood, awkwardly staring at Mardi.

"Why, Boone," Mardi spoke from across the table, "please sit down. We don't stand on needless formalities here. Do we, Jemmy?"

Jemmy Jem laughed, and again, another spell was broken. "No ma'am, we sure don't. And that's the truth. Why if Mister Boone could see the ways you run around here sometimes. And how you runs down to the lake and what you's wearin'…or should I say *not* wearin'!" She cackled again, and Mardi blushed in her innocence.

"You hush up, Jemmy. Don't be tellin' all my secrets." Mardi covered her mouth with her fingertips in a gesture of shyness, and then lowered her eyes to the table and the place setting in front of her. The luster of Boone's pieces caught her and drew her out of herself. She forgot everything that had transpired and felt herself being seduced, almost made love to, by the honesty of his work. The graceful reality of his art embraced her with a sense of security and warmth. Suddenly, she felt she could tell Boone anything, and he would surely understand. She traced her fingertips across the sheen of her dinner plate, and in that moment, her embarrassment fled. "How beautiful your things are, Boone." She looked up, along the full length of the table, and met his eyes. "So filled with life…with a love of all that's alive."

Boone's heart raced once more, blood coursing deliriously through his veins. "Thank you, Mardi. I've never seen my things in such a fine setting. They look more wonderful than I ever thought they could." He held up his plate, turning it in the candlelight. "Do you see the grasshopper? I tried to blend it to the glaze so's if to seem it were not there at all. Like a ghost."

Mardi slowly spun her plate in her hands. "Yes, I see it now. Why, he's barely there."

Boone nodded. "It's like many things of life. Maybe *all* of life. We're barely here. Just hangin' on to a leaf or a blade of grass…or, in our case, another human being. Just to keep ourselves here. Holdin' on to each other to keep from disappearin' into the night."

A moment of silence hung in the room, suspended on Boone's words.

Jemmy Jem nodded appreciatively. "I knew you understood, Mister Boone. Now, it's time to eat." She took the tureen from the sideboard, ladled a rich, creamy soup into Mardi's bowl, then crossed the room and filled Boone's. "How fine this here soup looks in yer bowls, Mister Boone," she said. "I hope you enjoy it. It's an old Jamerson family recipe, a snapper soup with just a touch a' Jamaican curry powder in it."

Boone looked down at his filled soup plate. "I'm sure I will, Jemmy." He put a spoon to the soup, and with his first sip realized just how delicious it was. "This is right fine soup," he said, and proceeded to devour it all, ravenously, almost wolflike.

Jemmy chuckled. "I knew you was hungry, Mister Boone. Now you just wait till you try the roast beef. That's really gonna bring out the animal in you." She chuckled again. "Reynard," she said to the manservant, "carve that beautiful piece of meat whilst I pour some wine for Mister Boone and Miss Mardi." She filled a crystal goblet with a blood-red wine from a cut-glass decanter. "This here wine is something special, Mister Boone. We hope you like it."

Boone sipped at the blood of the grapes. "It's right fine," he said. "I ain't never had wine before, but I can tell this is right fine." He looked across the table at the vision in white at the far end. "It sort of tastes like the sun, Mardi. Both the earth and the sun at the same time." He sipped at his crystal glass again. "I can taste the warmth of some countryside in this here wine. And the light, too. But it don't taste like it's from here. It don't taste like it's from America."

Mardi sipped at her wine and smiled at Boone. "How perceptive of you, Boone. It's French wine. It comes from the fields of

Burgundy. And it's from the very last case we have left."

Jemmy chimed in, "We been savin' it for a special occasion, an I'd say that you and Miss Mardi may just as well drink up that whole dang case, Mister Boone, 'cause if this ain't a special occasion, I don't know *what* all is."

Boone finished the blood in his glass and laughed heartily. "I don't think we could, Jemmy. A whole case of wine? My lord!"

Mardi laughed little pearls into the air. "We could give it a try, Boone. If we had a mind to."

Boone looked across the burnished maple table and made his first advance. "Do *you*, Mardi? I'll join you…if you like."

Their eyes met, and the silence descended upon the room again. It held for but a moment, yet in that moment all things disappeared, except for the electricity that raced back and forth between Boone and Mardi. An electricity that carried a fierce heat at its core. The heat of newfound desire.

Jemmy Jem again broke the silence. "Stop it, you two. What in the name of the good Lord are y'all suggestin'? I meant you could drink that case o' wine over the course of time. There ain't no need to save it no more, the special occasion done arrived. But not all in one night!" She cackled loud and full from some place deep inside of her. "You two are crazy as a pair a' bobcats in heat. All in one night? I declare! Y'all are just a couple a' wild things, ain't you? Just wild in the night." She cackled again, and Reynard picked up the laughter and boomed his own happiness into the room. Boone and Mardi joined in and the room was filled with delight. A joy that seemed to bring a smile even to the portraits of Mardi's ancestors that hung on the dining room walls. Boone thought he heard, ever so softly, the sound of a harpsichord playing a charming little melody, floating gaily in from the library.

"Reynard, let's serve that roast beef before these two wild children *starve* to death," Jemmy Jem roared through the laughter. She refilled the crystal goblets with the blood-red wine, laughing all the while.

THIRTY-THREE

An overflowing plate of rare roast beef, vegetables, and mashed potatoes was placed in front of Boone. "Enjoy it, sir," Reynard said as he stepped back from the table. "I hope the taste of the food approaches the fineness of your plates."

"Thank you, Reynard," Boone said. "But couldn't we have some more light in the room? I like to be able to see what I'm eatin'." He spoke across the table: "Mardi, why don't we light the other candles on the table? I want to be able to see you, too."

Mardi, glowing with an inner radiance, looked imploringly at Jemmy Jem. "We could light the other candles, couldn't we, Jemmy? We could light them now."

Jemmy smiled. "I believe we could, Miss Mardi," Jemmy said softly. "I believe the life is back." Jemmy nodded to Reynard, who put a match to the candles. "Now, you eat that meat, Mister Boone," Jemmy said maternally. "We needs you to keep your strength up."

Boone cut into his beef, and it was as delicious as it looked in the now bright candlelight. "This is right fine beef," he said through a stuffed mouthful. And after he had done trencherman's work to half his plate he finally looked up and said, "Mardi, why was only one candle lit? And that in front of me?"

Mardi had set to her dinner almost as ravenously as Boone, and she ate with a gusto that brought a smile to Jemmy Jem's face. Her little girl was happy again. Mardi rested her knife and fork on the yellow-ware plate before her and looked at the portraits hung about the room. A deep sigh emerged from her, from somewhere hidden in her memory. "Before, there were always five bright candles all in a row."

"Before what?" Boone asked.

Sadness filled Mardi's eyes. "Before, when there was life in this room. When there were people in this room, not just pictures on the walls. When things were alive in all of this house, and in my heart as well." She became silent, lapsing back into the warmth of those memories.

Jemmy spoke softly to Boone. "Before the war, Mister Boone." Boone nodded, understanding Mardi's loss.

"You see, Boone," continued Mardi, "my mama believed all our lives should burn with an inner fire. And as a constant reminder, she placed a candle on the table before each of us." Mardi pushed her chair back from the table, and Reynard, as quick as his namesake fox, moved behind it to assist her, holding her arm as she rose to her feet. Mardi glided to a large family portrait on one of the walls. "Here they are, Boone. My family. My beloved family," and she began to point to each figure. "This is my father, Charles Everett Jamerson. He was a good man. A generous man. With a quiet strength and a great inner dignity. He knew things, Boone. He knew about the cycles of life and nature. He knew about the energy in the sun and the coolness of the moon. And he loved the land. Oh, my, how he loved our plantation land here at Meadow Wood. He said the land was everything, every blade of grass was a miracle. I believe he would have liked you, Boone. I believe he would have seen some of himself in you."

Boone was deeply touched. "Thank you, Mardi. He sounds like a fine man. I'm sure he was a wonderful father to you."

"To all of us, Boone. We all loved him. And none more than my mama. Her name was Susanna and she came from the Clark family." Mardi gestured to a grouping of people on the far side of the room. "That's my grandma and grandpa over there. My mother is the little girl in that portrait." Mardi pointed back to the Jamerson family picture. "And here she is as a grown woman with her children. Isn't she just a lovely woman?"

"She's very pretty," Boone said.

"And there are all my brothers and sisters. This is Virgil and Aaron. They're twins, and they were the firstborn. This is my oldest sister, Lucretia. And this is Lilibeth, the next oldest. That's me, the youngest daughter. And there's Charles Junior, the youngest of us all. Look here in the corner of the portrait,

Boone. This is our dog. He's a springer spaniel and his name is Beauregard. We called him Beau, of course. Charles Junior and I used to wrestle with him and run down to the lake, trying as hard as we could to keep up with him. He just loved to swim in the lake. When I learned how, I would swim with him. We'd go from one end to the other and back. It was wonderful."

"From one end to the other? And back? I hope that lake isn't too big, Mardi. You could of drowned."

Mardi laughed her bells into the air. "Oh, Boone. I'm a good swimmer. And the lake's not *that* big. You'll see."

"I'd like to see you swim in that lake, Mardi." Boone skewered the last forkful of his beef, and then finished his wine. "What happened to everybody? Did they all run off because of the war? Is that why only one candle is lit?"

"Jemmy," Mardi said, "I'd like another glass of wine, please. And see that Boone's glass is refilled as well." She smiled. "After all, we have an entire case to consume."

Boone laughed, secure and happy in such a grand setting. He was a contented man that evening.

Mardi quietly glided back to her place at the table. Reynard deftly tilted her chair out, waited for her to settle in her seat, and gracefully slid her before her place setting.

"Thank you, Reynard." She sipped at her wine and picked up with her story. "About the candles, Boone. You see, when we ate in here, they were all lit. But I always wondered why there were only five. And one day at dinner, I said to mama, 'You and Daddy sit on each end of the table and you each get your own candle. But that only leaves three for the rest of us. We have to share a candle...and I want my own, just like you. I want my own candle, too.' I was such a silly child. So carefree and unknowing. And my mama, in her wisdom and her goodness, told me, 'Mardi, in each flame, as in your own lives, you will all find something special, seen only by you. But you will find that the flame, and your life, will be much brighter if you have someone to share it with. I want you children to share your light with each other, until one day that special person comes along. Then you will share the fire in your hearts with your one true love. Just as your father and I have shared our fire together. All you children are the result of that flame of love. Someday, I hope you will all know the intensity of that flame.' And then, Boone, she smiled at all of us, with such a love in her eyes that I thought I would just melt like the candle wax."

Boone was touched by Mardi's story. "How sweet your mother is. What a fine way to tell her children about love."

"There was love everywhere here at Meadow Wood. And everyone who worked here was treated with respect. You see, we were not like other Southern families. True, we had colored fieldworkers and house servants, and they were not paid wages. But they were provided with ample food and comfortable rooming. In fact, father was preoccupied with reuniting families which had been splintered by being sold into bondage to, well…less compassionate slaveholders. Our workers were not segregated by sex, they were housed as kin. Prosperity and cooperation were abundant, without so much as a petty quarrel. Anger just did not have a place to root itself in this atmosphere. And because of the love we shared here at Meadow Wood, everything seemed to thrive. The crops and the cotton were aplenty and the livestock grew fat. There was laughter everywhere, from the Jamerson family to all the workers and field hands. There was always plenty of food to eat and corn liquor to drink and singing and dancing at night after a hard day's work." Mardi stopped, reliving those days of joy in her mind's eye. A sweet silence hung in the air.

"It sounds wonderful, Mardi," Boone said. "It sounds like it was almost paradise."

"It *was*, Mister Boone," Jemmy Jem said. "It was as if the good Lord had given us everything we needed. We didn't want fer nothin'. But we never had too much, neither. The sins of gluttony and avarice never reared they ugly heads here at Meadow Wood. We always had just enough. Just enough to make us all happy. Like you said, Mister Boone, almost paradise." Jemmy closed her eyes to hide a tear of memory.

"Then what happened?" Boone asked. "Where is everybody?"

"The war happened, Mister Boone," Jemmy said, wiping her eye with her apron. "The damned war."

"I remember being with my brothers, Virgil and Aaron," Mardi said. "I was sitting in the shade of a weeping willow by the lake and they were skipping stones across the water. And like they always did in those days, they were arguing about the war. Before that time, I had never seen them argue. I still remember nearly every word they spoke on that dreadful day."

"What was it all about?" asked Boone.

Mardi gulped at her glass of wine, as if to steel herself for the revelation, the tragic answer to Boone's question.

"Virgil spoke first," she said. "He asked Aaron, 'Well, which side do you think we should be on?' Aaron replied, 'No two ways about it. Come mornin', we'll ride north. To fight with the free men.' But that was not Virgil's mind. 'North?' he said. 'But all the action's west, round Shiloh and Corinth!' Aaron said right back, 'We have to fight for what's right, Virgil. We've got to help free the slaves.' 'Hell,' Virgil said, '*we've* got slaves!' 'Not so's you could tell,' said Aaron. 'Pa told 'em they could all leave. Only one young couple took him up on the offer. All the rest are stayin' right here.' Virgil grew angry. 'How can you propose to fight the South?' he asked, his eyes aflame. 'She's like a mother to us. How can we up and turn on all we've ever known?'"

Mardi held her glass up to Jemmy. "Please, Jemmy, more wine. I don't know if I can get through this without it." As Jemmy filled her mistress's glass, so too Reynard filled Boone's.

With her brace of the blood-red wine, Mardi continued. "Aaron just looked at Virgil, hard in the eyes. 'Suit yourself,' he said. 'Come sunup, I'm ridin' out. To join the Union forces.' Virgil clenched his hands into fists. 'Over my dead body,' he said. Aaron cockily replied, 'Like I said, suit yourself,' and he turned and walked away. But as he brushed past, Virgil threw him to the ground. Aaron slowly got to his knees, wiped the dirt off his face...and charged Virgil, knocking him back into the shallows of the lake. Oh, Boone, they fought like animals. My two brothers, the twins, clawing like two feral cats over a queen in heat. I ran off, calling for mama, hoping to get her to stop them before they killed each other."

Mardi took a long draw on her wine. Boone noticed that the harpsichord music he thought he had heard was now gone. "Did you find her?" he asked. "Was she able to stop them?"

"Not that time. By the time I got back with mama, Aaron had brought Virgil around to his way of seeing things." Mardi smiled, as if at some private joke. "But they didn't ride off to war for several weeks. In the course of his persuasion, it seems Aaron broke Virgil's arm."

Boone laughed and held his wine glass up in a toast. "Fine vittles, Jemmy. My best regards to the cook."

"I'm the cook, Mister Boone. Ain't no one left but Reynard an' me," Jemmy said.

Boone looked quizzically across the table at Mardi. "Mardi, you said your pappy offered your coloreds their freedom but none took him up. How come Jemmy Jem and Reynard are the only two still here at Meadow Wood?"

THIRTY-FOUR

As the harpsichord music seemed to have disappeared, so too was the joy and happiness beginning to slip from the room. A darkness was descending on Mardi, but she felt compelled to continue with her story of the Jamerson family.

"When Virgil's arm finally mended, my brothers did travel north." She sighed from the place in her memory where her sadness resided. "Oh, Boone. How strange are the workings of fate. Those two handsome men, my big brothers, never even made it out of the county before they were arrested. The doctor who set Virgil's arm had spread word of their fight and of their plans to enlist in the Union Army. They were arrested as traitors and shipped off to Belle Island prison near Richmond. Inside of three months, they died of scurvy and starvation, clutched tight in each other's arms."

Jemmy gave out a muffled cry of anguish as Mardi stared in silence at the flame of life dancing on the tip of her candle. Reynard then picked up the story. "Mistrah Charles and I took a wagon to Richmond to fetch the bodies of the twins. I told the massah' he didn't have to go, that I would bring the boys home. But he insisted, and he never said a word on the way out nor on the way back. Every once in awhile, I'd hear him crying, softly to his self. We buried the boys in the family house in the cemetery in La Fayette. The reverend what did the ceremony was a good friend of Mistrah Charles and he did a right fine sermon for the boys. He said they would always be with us. In our hearts."

Jemmy spoke up through her tears. "I feel as if Aaron and Virgil are watchin' us now. And they's happy you is here, Mister Boone. Here for Miss Mardi."

Mardi came out of her trance. "That night, after the burial, I recall mama said not a word throughout our dinner. Her eyes seemed dead, and she just stared into the burning candle before her. Then she reached out to it, and with her bare fingers, she slowly pinched the wick, snuffing out the flame. She rose from her chair, and without a word to any of us, left the room. I knew then there was something terribly wrong with her."

"How great her grief must have been," Boone said. "To lose her firstborn boys. And so needlessly."

"The war, Mister Boone," Jemmy said. "The war makes for a kind of madness that comes over peoples. It causes things to happen that are without reason. Things that belong to the house of the devil."

"Just before midnight," Mardi continued, "my little brother Charles Junior found mama in the barn. Hung dead by the neck."

"Oh my Lord," Boone gasped.

"From that day on, we never laughed again," Mardi said. And the crops didn't seem to grow with the abundance they once had. Just barely, as if the joy of life had been removed from Meadow Wood. The litters were small, the eggs few. I suppose the fire had gone out of everything. Papa was just a shell. He was here, but there seemed to be nothing of a man inside."

She took another sip of her wine, the blood-red wine of Burgundy. The last of the wine in the Jamerson cellar. "One day, I don't know how much later, they came. A corps of Union cavalry, charging like hellhounds out of the morning mist. Beasts. And the madness had overtaken all of them. Some held fiery torches, and the sound of horse's hooves on the cobblestones was a clatter that sent a panic rising through us all. Men leapt from their mounts and they battered down the front door. The children and the servants were all screaming as those blue soldiers flooded into the foyer, guns held high and at the ready. My father greeted them from the top of the stairs with blasts from his repeating rifle. He killed half a dozen, maybe more, as he came down the stairs, firing all the while. They shot him dead as his feet touched the stone of the ground floor.

"Next, they came for us. My two sisters were in a bedroom upstairs. The soldiers broke down the locked door and proceeded to rape them both. Only when too many of the men had taken their turn, did they cut their throats. Charles Junior came at them with an axe, but just as he buried that axe head into the back of a soldier, he was blown off his feet by a rifle blast that tore a hole through his chest. The bastard Yankee, for good measure, then stabbed him with his bayonet, over and over. Like a vicious, evil creature that had lost all sense of decency. All sense of humanity."

"How is it that you escaped?" asked Boone.

"We have a secret room off the library. Behind a bookcase that pushes inward within one wall. Papa kept his papers and special things in there. When the soldiers rode up, I had been practicing the harpsichord, and I saw them through the window. I saw them shoot Papa, and then I hid in the secret room. I heard everything, Boone. Everything." She put her hands over her ears, as if to blot out the horrific sounds of her memory.

"They ran through the house, looting whatever they liked, destroying what they'd no need for. Outside, some of our workers tried to defend Meadow Wood, but those Yankee beasts shot them down. Our men with their pitchforks and scythes were no match for armed soldiers. The remaining families ran for their lives as the blue-bellied bastards burned their living quarters to the ground.

"When they had their fill, the soldiers rode off as quickly as they had come, leaving nothing but death and destruction behind. I came out of my hiding place and saw all that had happened. Boone, I shall never wipe the sight of that horror from my eyes." Mardi covered her face with her hands and began to weep, her body racked with sobs as her anguish consumed her.

Boone was so moved by her sorrow that he rose from his chair and crossed the room to her. He stood above her, hesitated for a moment, and then knelt and took her in his arms. "Hush, Mardi. Hush now," he said as he stroked her hair. "Everything is all right. They're all in Heaven, now."

Mardi threw her arms around Boone, holding him tight and close. "Oh, Boone, I do hope so. I do." Boone could feel her heart throbbing wildly in her chest, like the trilling heart of a bird, and he was even more moved. He continued to stroke her hair, feeling the litheness, the suppleness of her body in his arms. She was lean and hard, like a young animal, yet she was also delicate, and finely boned. Her golden hair was as soft as silk thread. And her breasts, pressing against him, were full and firm and Boone realized he was becoming aroused. And he wanted her.

"That's right, Mister Boone," Jemmy Jem said. "You comfort Miss Mardi. That's what she's been needin'. Some strong arms to hold her. That's why you're here." Jemmy looked at Reynard and smiled. He answered with a grin and nod of his own. "She needs you, Mister Boone. She surely does."

THIRTY-FIVE

Reynard led Boone up the grand staircase. It was long past midnight and Boone had had too much of the Burgundy wine. Mardi had told him many stories of her life at Meadow Wood and she had laughed and cried far into the night. Boone had held her hand and stroked her hair and laughed and cried with her as she confided all her joys and hopes and fears. It was as if she hadn't talked to anyone in far too long a time, and all her pent-up desires and memories came rushing out, engulfing Boone in wave after wave of emotion. By the end of the evening, he felt drained, but he had never wanted a woman as feverishly as he wanted Mardi.

At the top of the stairs, Reynard guided Boone to Mister Jamerson's bedroom. "The massah' slept here," Reynard said. "It's all yours now, Mister Dillard. I put some sleeping clothes on the chair next to the bed for you. If you need anything, just pull that bell cord by your pillow. I'll hear it." And with that, he slipped quietly out of the room.

Boone trudged to the bed, pulled off his shoes and stripped down to his underwear, tossing his borrowed clothes in a heap. He drank from a pitcher of water on the nightstand, and then collapsed on the luxurious, down-filled blankets that covered the bed of Charles Everett Jamerson, the master of Meadow Wood plantation.

Boone immediately fell into a deep and fitful sleep. A fire seemed to engulf him and he burned with the heat of the imagined blaze. Figures swirled like wraiths all around him, but he couldn't make out exactly what they were. But he could sense their presence, and they were evil. Suddenly, a bone-chilling cold seized him. The licks of flame that consumed him now burned like ice, and the ice entered his veins, chilling him to his core. Boone shivered with icy sweat as the malevolent creatures hovered about. Then he felt a pressure on his chest, as if one of them were sitting on him. He couldn't breathe. His lungs labored and sucked for air. Then something on the floor beside his bed began to pull at his hand. His arm slipped off the bed, as if clutched and yanked toward a black abyss, a place of unknowable fear. Boone felt a terrible dread as he gasped for air, fighting the weight of the thing upon his chest, while at the same time, struggling with the force that tugged him down into the terror of the dark. He somehow found his voice and cried out in his fear. "Cassy!" He bolted upright in bed. And in the utter darkness, he had no idea where he was. No idea if he were awake, or dead.

The door creaked open. A rush of panic shot through Boone. He feared the worst as a shadowy figure crept through the cracked door in the dimmest of light. A figure out of the darkness and out of his dream. It slithered across the room like an upright snake and Boone shuddered in his night-sweat. The figure came closer, then briefly passed through a trickle of moonlight slipping between the draperies. Boone's heart shed its icy grip and leapt with excitement. It was Mardi!

"I thought I heard you cry out, Boone. Someone's name. Are you all right?"

Boone rubbed his face, wiping off the fever beads and trying to clear his eyes. Was she really there, at the foot of his bed? Or was she an apparition, stepped forth from his nightmare? He tightly closed, and then slowly opened his eyes. And beside his bed, where the evil force had been pulling his arm, dragging him into a terrifying pit, stood Mardi. She wore a diaphanous white gown and the moonlight glinted through the sheer fabric. It was her only covering, and beneath it Boone could see the silhouette of her body.

She reached out and touched his arm. "I don't ever want you to be afraid, Boone. There's no reason for us to have any more fear. Not now…now that we're finally together." Mardi opened her gown and let it slip from her shoulders. And she stood naked before him, in the soft, silver gleam of the moon. She moved back the bed covers, and seeing Boone's underwear, giggled almost like a schoolgirl. "We can't do anything with those on," she said. Her laughter was pure and fresh and made Boone feel light and joyful, clearing his head of all the demons that had possessed him in his dream.

Mardi slowly pulled down Boone's shorts, and when her hand brushed across his member, it swelled with fullness. Mardi smiled, bent forward, and kissed it lightly on its crown. Boone shuddered with delight. "That's just for starters," she said. She stripped his shorts down his legs and over his feet, her silken blonde hair dancing along Boone's body. Perched on her knees, she kissed his legs as she moved up to his groin, and then began to lick Boone's manhood with her tongue. She wet it with her saliva and took it into her mouth. Boone moaned in ecstasy. Then he took Mardi by her shoulders and drew her up to him. "Let me kiss you," he said as her breasts rubbed along his body. "Let me kiss your mouth."

He enfolded her in his arms, their lips met, and Mardi's mouth hungrily opened to him. Her tongue flicked over his and Boone held her tight and firm, answering her tongue with darts and swirls of his own. Mardi trembled with a cat's purring and then Boone rolled her over. "I want you, Mardi," he said as he spread apart her thighs. He held back for a moment, as he took in her naked body, soft and open to him. "My God, you are a beautiful thing," he said.

He moved into her. Slowly and easily, with great tenderness. Mardi sucked a sharp intake of breath, and expelled a muffled murmur of pain. "Have I hurt you?" Boone asked gently.

"No, Boone...no. I've been waiting for this moment. Waiting so long." She began to cry with relief and rapture, her body shivered with pain and delight. And as she encircled Boone's back with her legs, pulling him deep inside her, Boone realized he was the first man that Mardi had ever known.

THIRTY-SIX

Brilliant sunlight spilled into Charles Jamerson's bedroom, the light of a fine Georgia day. A rap on the door woke Boone. He groggily raised his head from the pillow, but before he could find his voice, the door swung open and Reynard poked his head into the room. "Miss Mardi extends an invitation for lunch on the veranda," he said. Without awaiting a reply, he withdrew and closed the door.

Boone's fingers tried to rub the sleep from his eyes. When he took his hands away, he stretched an arm out to feel for Mardi next to him. She wasn't there. And then he realized what Reynard had said. Of course she wasn't in bed with him, she was waiting for him to join her on the veranda for lunch. But he hadn't felt her get up from the bed, and he hadn't heard her leave the room. Had he slept so long and so deeply? He looked down at the floor, where Mardi had let her white nightgown fall from her shoulders. Where it had slipped from her naked body. But it wasn't there. Boone began to wonder if Mardi had ever come to his bed at all. Was the intense pleasure he had felt from making love to her, the passion of their intertwined bodies, the heat of their young flesh, merely part of a dream? Simply the opposite dimension of his nightmarish fear, the reverse side of the horror he had seen within the darkness?

He leapt from the bed, dressed quickly, and raced down the great staircase. He had to see her. He had to know if their night together had been real. Boone passed through open double-doors onto the expansive, lushly planted terrace at the rear of the manor. No one was in sight. The wrought-iron and glass table was completely bare. Lunch? How could we have lunch?

he thought.

And then he saw her. Only her head, bobbing and floating, as if disembodied. She was beyond a boxwood hedge rimming the veranda and a chill shot through Boone. Then she moved into view and Boone released a sigh of relief. She was riding the black stallion that had pulled her carriage, and trailing the reins of a fine, dappled roan.

"Well, it's about time, Boone Dillard," she called out to him. "I thought I was going to starve to death before you ever woke up."

Boone could only stammer, overwhelmed by her beauty. She was a vision in white riding clothes on a sleek black mount. "Mardi...I...did we...?"

Mardi laughed. "Did we what, silly. Did we leave the earth? Did all time stop? Did we create a new existence with our bodies?" She dropped the reins of the dappled horse and turned the stallion. "I'll race you to the lake. Lunch awaits, Mister Dillard." And with that, she dug her heels into the ribs of the black horse and galloped off across the great lawn, disappearing into the seemingly impenetrable woods.

Boone rushed down the stone steps leading from the veranda. He leapt onto the dappled roan and rode off in hot pursuit of his vision that had just vanished into the green wall.

He raced across the grounds and came to a small trail into the woods. "So that's how she did it," he said to himself. He headed his steed into the green, through the Spanish moss and between fat trunks of towering Georgia pine.

He rode down the winding trail but could see nothing of Mardi, nor could he hear the hoofbeats of her black stallion. He galloped along, branches whipping at him, seeming to grab him. To hold him back from his rendezvous. But he raced on, into the wilderness, hell-bent for his destiny. Yet there was no sign of her. No clue to her whereabouts, or even her existence.

At last, he came to a clearing and saw a trail of deep hoofprints in the soft ground. He followed the impressions until coming suddenly upon Mardi's horse, standing with empty saddle, reins tied to a low-hanging limb. Beyond the horse, Boone saw the lake. A warm wind rippled the inviting blue water. Mardi was nowhere to be seen.

"Mardi!" he called out. "Where are you?" There was no reply.

He walked to the shore of the lake, scanned the surface, and called again. "Mardi!" Then the ripples spread wide and Mardi's head emerged from the depths, again seemingly disembodied. "Here I am," spoke the head. It smiled sweetly as it glided through the blue toward Boone. At the water's edge, the head rose from the lake, revealing the rest of Mardi attached to it. Complete in bodily form once more, she stepped softly through the shore grass, lithe and radiant, and naked. Boone stepped ankle-deep into the lake, holding out his hand to this goddess that came to him, all moist and glistening.

"I need you," she whispered as she snaked her arms around his neck. She pressed her body close to his and kissed him full and deep on the mouth. He returned her kiss with a frenzy of his own, enfolding her in his arms. He lifted her off her feet and stepped back out of the water, setting her down on the damp shoreline. Mardi's hands moved to unclasp Boone's belt buckle. "Make love to me, Boone," she said. "Right here, on the wetness of the earth. Love me like you did last night." She looked into his eyes, imploringly. "Right here, on the wetness of our mother."

THIRTY-SEVEN

Afterward, they sat in the shade of a great weeping willow, lazing upon a blanket, savoring a fine lunch emptied from Mardi's saddlebags, and another bottle of the Burgundy wine.

Boone stretched himself like a cat in the mottled light. The sun was now high in the sky and the warmth of the day enveloped the two lovers in a lushness of sensuality. "I've never felt so good," Boone said. He reached his hand out to Mardi, taking hers as he lay back on the blanket. Her hand was warm and soft in his, and Boone could feel the beating of her heart in her cupped palm. "I feel as if nothing matters, only the two of us, here and now," he said. He looked up through the branches of the willow into the high Georgia sky, into the dazzling light of the sun.

"It should always be us, Boone," Mardi said as she snuggled against him, resting her head on his chest. "I love being here with you. This is my favorite place in the world. This lake, this big willow. I always came here as a child." Then she giggled, not unlike a child. "But of course, I never before did what *we* just did." She kissed him on the chest and neck. Kisses that felt to Boone as if dew-moistened flowers were being brushed across his body. I'm so happy you're here now, Boone. Finally here." She kissed his lips, softly and delicately, like a butterfly floating on a breeze.

Then she sat up and looked out across the lake. Into the empty space that held her ghosts. They came to her again, possessed her, and her eyes went vacant as she spoke. "It all started right here. For my family, the war began the day my brother Virgil threw down upon his twin, Aaron." She pointed to the shore. "Right over there, where we made love. That was the very spot where the fighting began." She turned back to Boone. "And I feel that your being inside of me on the wetness of our Mother Earth somehow cools their madness. I feel that our love somehow forgives the sin of their anger."

Boone reached out and touched Mardi on the delicate curve of her shoulder. Her skin was soft and white under his rough, country hand, and he loved the contrast of her flesh against his. "I'm sure their sins are forgiven them, Mardi," he said comfortingly. "God forgives everything. He loves us all. He only wants our happiness." Boone moved his hand across her back, softly and with great tenderness. "That's why we're here, don't you think? To live in happiness?"

Tears began to fill Mardi's eyes. She was overwhelmed by the emotions racing through her. "Oh, Boone. From that terrible day, my family has only known death. I come here most every day, for I have to believe, by some means in all creation, there must be a way to return to that wholeness. That happiness." She wiped at her tears. "But every time I ride away, my spirit cries. My family is dead. We are no more."

Boone sat up from the blanket and took her in his arms. He spoke softly to her, as if speaking to a child. "I don't know about that, Mardi. I tend to find the dead are not powerless. In some ways, they're still with us. They'll always be with us. I'd have to confide, the mysteries of the spirits are just about the most magical part of life. They are wonderful, and far beyond the blood of our knowledge."

Mardi hugged him tightly. "Boone, my Boone. I knew you'd understand." He kissed the top of her head as she pressed herself into his chest. Clinging to him with all her strength, as if she were trying to absorb his courage, his very essence.

"Just hold me," she said. "Let me feel your warmth. The warmth of your living flesh. The beating of your heart." She squeezed him even harder. "Crush me into you, Boone. Make me disappear into you."

Boone held her close, captivated by her delicacy and her need of him. But he dared not embrace her with all his might, for she was like a bird in his arms, so soft and wanting and lovely.

He did not know how long he held her that way. The Earth turned in its perpetual spin along its prescribed arc around the sun, and the day ventured slowly but inevitably into the future.

The warmth of that Georgia plantation lulled Boone into an almost hypnotic state. Nothing seemed to matter but the woman in his arms and the sweetness of the moment he had entered into. Time became infinite, and it lost all meaning.

Finally Mardi spoke. "Do you believe things are possible, Boone? Things that are beyond our senses? Beyond what we can hold true in our everyday reality?"

"I reckon I do, Mardi. It seems just about anything is possible. If we want it bad enough."

"I believe that, too," Mardi said. She pulled back from Boone's protective embrace and looked deeply into his eyes. "I believe there is an energy that can be manipulated for our good. For the good of everything. It's the energy that supports this planet and all life on this planet. It's God's energy and it's our energy. We can make it do whatever we want, if we believe…and if we understand it."

Boone turned from her intense gaze and looked out over the eternal blueness of the water. "But only if we do it for love, Mardi. If we do it for evil, that is the ultimate sin. I believe that anything is possible in the name of love."

Mardi stroked his hair and looked out over the lake, following Boone's eyes, into infinity. "I love you, Boone," she whispered.

THIRTY-EIGHT

The days and nights passed in a delirium. They ate and drank, laughed and told stories, sang songs as Mardi played the harpsichord again, swam in the lake, rode horses, explored the plantation grounds, and made love for hours. Boone was intoxicated with a rapturous delight, and Mardi was once again enthralled with life, laughing through the days and far into the night.

And there was hardly a thought of Coker Creek Hollow. Only a vague remembrance of a promise once spoken.

One evening, as Boone lay in sudsy water in an enormous tub in Charles Jamerson's bathroom, Mardi came to him. "That tub is more than large enough for two, Mister Dillard," she said. "Mind if I join you?" She untied her plush cotton robe and let it slip to the floor, just as she had let her diaphanous nightgown fall from her shoulders on their first night of lovemaking, and once again, she was naked.

She stepped lightly over the edge of the tub and eased herself down into the hot water, facing Boone. "My, you like it *hot*, Mister Dillard."

Boone chuckled. "I reckon I do, Miss Jamerson."

He spread his legs to the side of the tub to accommodate her as she gingerly slipped herself in. The heat of the water was intoxicating to her. She found her feet were just at the level of Boone's member and she coyly took it between them and softly began to tease it to life. Boone closed his eyes in pleasure and reached his hands under the water to Mardi's legs, caressing them.

"I've never made love in a bathtub before," he said.

Mardi giggled. "I never made love *anywhere* before you came along." Gently, her feet clamped tighter and quickened their work. Boone's pulse began to race as he was overcome with desire for her.

"I do believe you have made me ready to love you this instant, Mardi." He clasped his hands around her slender thighs, spreading them as he pulled her to him. But Mardi stiffened her legs and put her feet against his stomach, resisting his pull. "Just a minute, Mister Dillard. I don't make love to men with prickly hairs on their faces."

Boone ran a hand across his face, feeling his day's stubble. "I didn't shave this morning." He laughed. "And it's all your fault, Miss Jamerson. I seem to recall you were the one who wanted to see the sun rise from the hill beyond the lake. And I do believe we barely had time to get dressed before we had to ride off into the night to see the first light of dawn."

"I stand accused," Mardi said. "But wasn't it lovely? Wasn't it worth it?"

Boone nodded. "I don't think I've ever seen anything so…holy, before. Like the first light in the Garden of Eden. It was so pure. So alive."

Mardi softened. "Boone, you are my man." She relaxed her legs, moved to him, and kissed his cheek. "But I will not let that porcupine face make love to me."

"If you'll hand me that razor and cup of lather soap," Boone said, "I'll shave my quills for you."

"No," Mardi said. "I will." She reached over the tub to a small table that held an ivory-handled straight razor and one of Boone's yellow-ware mugs that was now doing duty as a shaving-soap receptacle, with a carved-ivory brush propped within. Mardi lathered the soap and painted Boone's face with white foam. "That's how you'll look when we're old and gray," she said. "And I'll love you even then."

She opened the carved-ivory straight razor. "I do hope this is sharp. I wouldn't want to nick that pretty face." She ran her finger along the blade's edge. "Oh, my. It's sharp all right." Then she put the razor to Boone's cheek.

"Now you be careful," Boone said. "You ever done this before?"

Mardi laughed her little bells into the warm steamy air of the bathroom. "You mean, have I ever sat naked in a tub with a man and touched him where my feet touched you? And let him do to me what you, Mister Dillard, are going to do to me after I finish your shave? Is that what you mean?"

"I reckon not," Boone replied.

"I have never done anything with *any* man before you," Mardi said. "But I watched my father shave many times, and I have always thought it unfair that women can't grow beards, for they are denied the pleasure of shaving."

Boone chuckled. "I don't know if I'd call shaving a pleasure, you silly thing."

"Well, the lather is so white and fluffy, like whipped cream. The razor is so elegant in its simplicity. And my father always hummed a little song to himself as he shaved, so he must have been enjoying himself."

"Then your father was a happy man," Boone said.

Mardi looked into his eyes. "And are *you* a happy man, my love?"

"I am happy beyond the right of a mortal man." Boone kissed her lightly on the nose, leaving it foamy white with lather. "I have been enchanted by a pixie from the forest."

Mardi smiled, and inside her chest, her heart surged with joy at Boone's response. "Then let this pixie do her work. You can trust me, Boone. I would never hurt you."

Stroke by stroke, Mardi slowly worked the razor over Boone's face. Her touch was as light as an angel's wings and the blade drew not a nick. "Now lift your head," she said after she had finished his features. "I need to do your neck."

"I'd be grateful if you would be most careful with that part," Boone said. "Unlike my happiness, my blood is still mortal."

"As is mine, my love."

Boone tilted back his head and Mardi carefully ran the razor across his throat, smoothly whisking away the porcupine quills. When she had stroked off the last of the lather, she rinsed the blade under the water and smiled at Boone as her fingers traced his silken face. "There you are, my handsome prince. My deliverer."

Boone returned the smile. Her touch was as soft as a summer breeze flowing over him. It was almost immaterial, without substance, yet it was fully there, warm and sensate. He felt a great desire welling up, a desire to possess and devour this delicate creature before him. Boone clutched at her hand, held it tight in a kind of frenzy, and kissed it deeply with a fevered hunger. As his lips were pressed to her hand, Mardi's other hand—clutching the cleansed razor—suddenly broke the foamy surface. And in the flash of an instant she drew the blade sharply across his neck, cutting into the flesh just beneath his jaw. As blood began to seep from the slash along Boone's throat, she held the stained razor up before his eyes. Boone reacted neither with shock nor fear, but his steely gaze bore questioningly into her eyes.

Mardi then raised the blade to her own throat. Boone reached to stop her, but before he could, she sliced her flesh. Her precious blood flowed from the shallow gash, pooled in the cup of her collarbone, then trickled between her breasts. She tossed aside the razor, reached out, and curled her fingers around a thatch of Boone's hair. Pulling him to her, she pressed her bleeding wound against the cut on Boone's throat. They nuzzled together, neck to neck, like wolves in some feral ritual. Mardi's teeth gnawed at Boone's ear, their blood intermingled and smeared their bodies, dripping down into the reddening tub water.

Mardi's lips moved to Boone's neck. She licked at his wound, and then sucked blood from it. Her stained, burgundy-red mouth then met Boone's. She kissed him hard, her passion hot as burning coals. And he returned her fever, lost in their all-consuming heat.

Mardi pulled back for just an instant. "I know you've come for me," she said. "I know because I've called to you in my dreams, and you have answered my call. It's no longer a dream, Boone. Now, you possess my body and soul. No matter what the cost, you I must keep. Forever."

She closed her eyes, and still grasping Boone's hair, brought his mouth to the gash along her slender neck. In his abandonment, Boone sucked the blood with a savage thirst. And in his eyes, everything went red.

THIRTY-NINE

The Earth continued to revolve on its axis and it was now midsummer. On a steamy morning, Jemmy Jem looked down from an upstairs window, holding a newly hatched chick in her palm. She gently stroked its downy yellow back as she smiled at the two lovers below.

Outside the mansion, Boone and Mardi walked down the front steps of the manor, linked arm-in-arm, looking for all the world like a newly married bride and groom. At the foot of the great stairway, Reynard held the reins of the dappled roan which Boone had become accustomed to riding on their jaunts through the countryside.

"You won't be long, will you, Boone?" Mardi asked, trying to stifle back a tear.

Boone lovingly touched her cheek. "Ain't but a chore or two to look after, sweetheart. There's no need for tears. I'll be back before the light changes. I promise."

Boone took the reins from Reynard and mounted the horse. Mardi grabbed his leg, clinging to it.

"Boone, don't leave me," she said with a touch of panic in her voice. "These past weeks have filled me with a lifetime of joy. I couldn't bear to lose you."

Boone smiled down at Mardi. "Oh, my little one. I'm not going to leave you." He leaned low in the saddle and kissed her wet cheek. "Mardi, I've never known such pleasures. I can't believe such a place as this even exists. It can only be paradise. And you, my angel, are God's sweetest creation."

Boone spurred the horse to action and turned it away from the mansion, clopping slowly down the cobblestones. He looked back over his shoulder at the wraithlike figure in white taffeta, waving back at him.

"I'll be back before sundown, Mardi," he called.

"I'll be here for you, Boone," came her reply. "I'll *always* be here for you!"

Boone smiled to himself and broke the roan into a gallop, racing off down the broad *allée* of oaks.

At the second-story window, Jemmy Jem smiled beatifically, the peeping chick still cuddled on her open palm. She raised her other arm, around which was coiled a thick, black snake. The serpent stretched its gaping mouth and hissed. Its forked tongue darted as it struck at the chick, snaring it between bared fangs, before swallowing the tiny, fluttering bird whole.

FORTY

Boone rode into the town of La Fayette. It was a quiet day on the streets, almost too quiet. As if the war hadn't affected La Fayette at all. Boone wondered if the whole damn thing might not just be over with. And then he thought of Jebber. Perhaps nothing had happened to him. Perhaps the war had ended before his big empty head had become separated from his body by cannon shot, or his heart ripped open by rifle fire or bayonet. Perhaps he was still wearing his plumed hat and riding his horse back to Jewel, to show off to her what a great soldier he had become. He smiled to himself at the thought of his brother-in-law in his cavalry finery, waving his Yankee saber, and Jewel finally feeling proud of her man.

Boone hitched his horse at the square where he had first set out his wares in what now seemed to him another lifetime. He walked through the green park as people strolled by in languid movement paced for the heat of the now summer days. There was an ease and grace to the rhythms of the town, and Boone quickly became more certain than ever that the great conflagration was over. As he walked, Boone found that people were smiling at him and nodding his way. A few men tipped their hats, saying, "Morning, Mister Dillard." "Good day, Mister Dillard." Boone was stunned by this recognition. He passed two women seated on a park bench and heard one say, "Why, that's Boone Dillard." A couple glided past, arm-in-arm, and the woman said to her companion, "That's the gentleman who made all that beautiful pottery that was displayed that day here in the park." "I know," replied the man, "his name is Boone Dillard."

Boone's chest swelled with pride. They knew him! Just like

the peddler-gnome had said, people knew his name! What was best, they even greeted him. He was no longer just a farmer from some backwoods hollow. He was somebody. Then he looked at his clothes and realized he was dressed as a man of substance. An important person. His pride swelled even more, and then began to slip over into vanity.

He strolled leisurely through the park, greeting people in his newly acquired hubris. He was thoroughly enjoying himself. There was only one more thing he had to do before he could completely enter this new life that had been created for him. He crossed the street to the shops opposite the town square, walking along, admiring the goods for sale, and turned into a fabric and sewing store. He moved down the narrow, musty aisle that was lined with shelves piled with bolts of cloth.

"May I help you, Mister Dillard?" the proprietor asked. He was a slight, frail man who had spent far too many years in the gloom of his shop. It was as if the man's skin had never seen sunlight, and held the same musty aura as his shop, which seemed never to have been exposed to fresh air.

"I want something fine," Boone said. "For my wife, Cassy. It's a promise I made."

"I have some beautiful silks here, sir. All the way from China. Came from before the war." One at a time, the man took down three bolts from the top shelf. The first was blue as the sky, another was lustrous gold, and the last was the red of fire. Boone had never seen such colors in a piece of cloth. The silk shimmered in the half-light of the shop, and the designs of the fabric were incredibly intricate weavings of hills and birds and flowers and mountains and geometrical patterns covering almost every inch of the cloth. Boone fingered the fabric. "How did they ever do this?" he asked the proprietor.

"I don't know, Mister Dillard. They're Chinese. They have mysteries we could never understand."

Boone nodded as an awareness of mysteries far nearer to him—in La Fayette—began to seep into his brain. "How do people know my name?" he asked.

The frail, almost transparent little man scratched at a boil on the back of his neck. "You're the man what made the beautiful pottery, ain't you?"

Boone nodded again.

"Well, they say yer name is Dillard. Boone Dillard." A silence hung in the air as Boone found himself unable to make a logical connection.

"But, I don't understand how."

"Sir," the proprietor said, "who can understand anything in these times?" The wizened, pale creature put a trembling hand on the sky-blue bolt of silk. "Now, which one would you like? And how many yards will do ya?"

"I want all of it," Boone said. "All three."

"How many yards, sir?"

"I said all of it," Boone barked. "Don't measure 'em, just crate 'em up. I'm shippin' all three to Tennessee. For my Cassy."

"All *three* will be expensive, sir. There's no more coming from China."

Boone drew a leather pouch from his coat pocket. It held the gold coins Jemmy Jem had paid him for his pottery.

Boone tossed three pieces of gold onto the counter. "I reckon this will cover it."

The gleam of profit flared up in the proprietor's eyes. "Yes sir, Mister Dillard. That will cover things nicely. What more would you like for your gold pieces?"

Boone shook his head. "Nothin' else. It's all for you. Just crate 'em."

The little man seemed to bounce with a jig. "Yes, sir! Yesiree," he said as he scurried to the back of the shop. "I got the box they come in right back here." He started to whistle a little tune.

He returned to the counter with a wooden crate that looked like a child's coffin. After wrapping each of the bolts of cloth in paper, he carefully laid them into the coffin. "That'll keep 'em nice and clean," he said to Boone. Then he moved the lid into place, but before he nailed it shut, Boone put out his hand.

"Hold it," he said. Boone cinched the leather bag tight by its drawstring and tossed the pouch of gold into the box where a child's head might lay. "Okay, close it up tight, mister."

The little man's eyes flashed again. "Is that all gold in that purse?"

"That's for my two boys," Boone said. "So they don't have to be farmers no more."

The proprietor grinned. "Lordy," he said, "all gold." He sealed the coffin with hammer and nails.

Boone lifted the crate by its rope handles and headed toward the door. He turned back and spoke into the gloom.

"Funny thing about gold," he said.

The proprietor's little fingers gripped his own gold coins tightly. "What's that, Mister Dillard?"

"It's like some kind of sorcerer's magic. Or maybe a witch's spell. It's got powers to change a man. Change him to the quick."

And Boone walked out of the dark shop, into the light.

FORTY-ONE

As Boone was securing the crate to the pack straps of the saddle on his horse, a commotion rose up in the streets. People ran from the park and out of the shops, gathering on the sidewalks, cheering and shouting and waving. Then Boone saw the reason for the cheers: a column of Confederate troops, marching down the street, led by none other than General Nathan Bedford Forrest and his court of foppish aides.

Boone pulled himself up on his horse and called out, "Gen'ral! Gen'ral Forrest!"

The general looked over, all regal and imperturbable. Boone cantered up and fell in alongside the column. "Gen'ral," Boone said. "Do you know what happened to Jebber?"

Forrest did not recognize Boone. "Jeb Stuart, is it, you're after?" Then he spat his disdain on the ground. "That gallivanting bastard."

"No sir, Gen'ral. Jebber *Stubbs*, my brother-in-law. The big ol' boy what killed that Yankee colonel with his bare hands and made off with his prized sword. You didn't hang us, remember?"

One of the fops, a dandified captain, spoke up. "The big one, sir. Strong as a bear and dumb as a mule." The other aides laughed condescendingly.

"Oh, that one," the general said. "I made him a lieutenant and sent him on up to Chattanooga. Seems he had his mind fixed on something he called 'big city.' I sent him to the nearest I could find with a company of men. I don't believe he could get himself into too much trouble in Chattanooga."

Boone was relieved. "Thank you, sir." But in that instant, something passed behind Boone's eyes. Some glimpse of things to come. "Beggin' yer pardon, sir, but does the name Chickamauga have anything to do with where Jebber's at?"

"It's the crick that runs into Chattanooga," the foppish captain said.

Boone looked to General Forrest. "There's blood there, sir. Lots of it."

The general recognized something in Boone's eyes. They had spoken of blood before. "Now I remember you," Forrest said. "You ran with that big ox, didn't you?"

"Like I said, sir, he's my brother-in-law."

The general looked Boone up and down, then peered closely at his face. "What happened to you, son?"

"Nothin', sir. New clothes, is all."

"I don't mean your clothes," Forrest said. "You look sick, boy. You got the fever?"

"No, sir. I'm fine. Never better. I come into a new situation, and I'm feelin' right fine," Boone said, smiling.

"You don't look fine. I'd see a doctor, son. You look like somethin' is bein' drawn out of you. A blood disease, I'd bet. Like you were slippin' away." And with that, General Forrest spurred his horse and rode off. His fops, in their slavish copying of the general's every gesture, followed close on his heels.

Boone brought the dappled roan to a halt, wondering what the general was talking about. He felt good. Strong. He'd never felt more alive, and he watched the troops file by with the townsfolk cheering, and saw they were not men, but boys. Fresh meat for the butcher's block of war. Boone realized the fighting was far from over. Then he thought of Mardi's brothers and all the boys dying across the nation for a cause brought on by nothing more than economic necessity. The South needed their slaves to keep the cotton industry in business, and they would invent any rationalization to maintain their financial advantage. Why, they would even go to war to keep their coloreds as slaves. And a bunch of slick-talking dandies in plumed hats would invent all kinds of reasons proclaiming why the South had to maintain its "traditions." They were all lies, Boone thought. Lies to keep their slaves. And now this column of boys was going off to die for those lies.

At the end of the column of walking dead followed a black wagon. It was piled with a white powder covered by a large tarpaulin. Boone recognized the powder spilling out of the wagon. He had seen it on the barge Jebber and he had taken at the beginning of their travels. It was quick lime. And driving the wagon was none other than the boatman, wearing his black cowl over his head. He looked over at Boone and smiled a toothless grin.

"Looks like you sold yer wares, son. Congratulations"

He snapped the reins over his horses—"Business ain't never been better fer me, neither."—and moved on, following the column through the streets of La Fayette, Georgia.

Boone and all the other citizens watched the new dead march down the main road. After they had finally disappeared from sight, Boone asked one of the cheering townsmen where he might post his box of silk.

"Well," the man said, "the post office is over across town, right next to the church." He pointed past the square, beyond the row of storefronts. "See the steeple rising in the sky? That's where you go. But to tell the truth, not much mail comes in nor out. There's a war on, ya' know."

Boone smiled. "Not so's I'd know. It don't seem to be hurtin' my life hardly at all."

"Well, then you're a lucky man, sir." He tipped his hat to Boone. "I wish you continued good fortune, Mister Dillard." The man turned and walked off, crossing the dusty main street of La Fayette. The street where a column of children in uniform had just passed.

Boone set his horse to a walk, heading for the church steeple, wondering again how so many people knew his name, but loving it, nonetheless.

FORTY-TWO

The post office was closed. And from the look of it—the gathered leaves and windswept dirt in the doorway—it had been closed for quite some while. Boone thought it would probably be closed for yet a long time to come. But perhaps the minister at the church could help him. He might know when the post office would be open. And he could hold the box until then, or until Jebber came back to town, looking for him. Boone hoped he would, and then Jebber could take the box back to Coker Creek Hollow along with his sword and fancy plumed hat. Wouldn't that make the folks back home happy!

Boone brought his horse about and walked it to the hitching rail in front of the white, steepled church. He dismounted and secured the reins, but before he could unlash the coffin box from the saddle straps, a figure in black emerged from the white doors. He thrust an arm out and pointed a finger at Boone. "You sir, stop!"

Boone froze, and then slowly turned about. A tall, gaunt man with sunken cheeks and hollow eyes, clad all in black save for a white collar, came down the steps in the shadow of the steeple. "In the name of God, man. What have you been up to?" he demanded of Boone.

Boone looked into his skeletal face—a skull set upon black-robed shoulders, skin pale as bone, and drawn back so tightly it seemed not to be there at all. The eyes, cavernous and unnaturally gray, seemed to look into Boone, to some place beyond his own eyes, deep into his very body. A chill ran through Boone, making him afraid of what those eyes were seeing.

Boone's throat was tight and dry, his voice strained. "Are you the parson of this here church?"

The man in black paid no heed to Boone's question. "The *mark* is upon you! You are *enveloped* by it. It *surrounds* you." His damning words came echoing from his skull, and they were harsh and reverberating, clanging in Boone's ears. "I ask you *again*, what have you been about?"

Boone's mind reeled, he felt a weakness in his knees and he held onto the saddle for support. "Mister, I…I just want you to take this box for me. Hold it until the post office opens. Or until my brother-in-law, Jebber Stubbs, comes for it. Comes lookin' for me."

"I will not *touch* that box," the skull said. "There is an *evil* about it. What does it hold?"

"Some silks for my wife," Boone stammered. "And gold coins for my boys. That's all. Ain't nothin' evil in that, Reverend."

The minister thrust his hand skyward. *"Render unto Caesar that which is Caesar's. And render unto God that which is God's."* He brought his hand down from its drift toward the heavens and pointed again, accusingly, at Boone. "How do you come by this gold?"

"From sellin' my wares, is all. I make pottery, and I sold the whole batch." Boone gestured back toward the square of La Fayette. "Everybody in town knows me, and they know of my things." Boone peered to find some glint of recognition within the skull's sunken eyes. "How come you don't know me?"

"I have tended my flock here in La Fayette for over twenty years, sir. I know the people, and *all* of what they know." His gray eyes bore into Boone, searching his depths. "I do *not* know you, sir, and I vouchsafe to say, the people of La Fayette do not know you, either."

"But they just spoke to me. They greeted me on the street. They called me by my name." Boone's voice began to shake with desperation. "They know who I am and they know the worth and beauty of my wares. Heck, the man in the shop where I bought the silks, he knew me, too."

The reverend shook his calciferous head. "My God, sir. You're mind is playing tricks on you. Can't you see? You've fallen prey to your own *dreams*. You've heard what you *wanted* to hear. And mark my words, you have never been spoken of by any Christian soul here in the city of La Fayette!"

Boone covered his ears as the minister's voice clanged and echoed again in his head. "It can't be," he said.

"You are marked. I thought it when I first saw you, and now I know it for certain. There is a possession upon you." The reverend laid a hand on Boone's shoulder. It held surprising warmth, and when next he spoke, his voice had lost its harsh, metallic note. "What have you been about, son? Tell me how you came by the gold?"

"Mardi bought all my wares," Boone replied. "And Jemmy Jem, she paid me with a purse full of gold. I been stayin' with them ever since. That's about all that's happened. 'Cept I love her. I do love Mardi."

The reverend's grip tightened on Boone and his gaze rose to the heavens. "Oh, Lord, I fear the worst." When at last his eyes fell back upon Boone, he asked, "Son, what is your name?"

"Boone. My name's Boone Dillard."

The reverend nodded. "Now tell me, Boone. This woman, Mardi, what is her surname?"

"Jamerson. Mardi Jamerson. She's the last of the Jamerson line."

The reverend closed his eyes and sucked in a deep gasp of air. "Oh, God in Heaven," he said as his breath spilled back out. He put both hands on Boone's shoulders. Steadying him. Holding him firmly like a ruined soldier before the surgeon's saw tears at a wasted limb. "Come with me, Boone. To the cemetery, just back of our church. I want you to *see* something." And there was now a fear in his voice.

FORTY-THREE

A centuries-old white oak shaded the church cemetery. The grounds were lushly planted and well tended, enclosed by ivied stonewalls.

"These souls have come before us," the reverend said to Boone, "and so too *we* will join them in the eyes of those who come after us."

The two men moved past grave markers, some settled and sunken, attesting to bodies long dead. They passed ornate statuary of angels and cherubs, elaborately carved blocks and pillars of marble—images and shapes of a hoped for afterlife to come. But there were also many raw graves with freshly turned earth and empty of statuary. These were the graves of the newly dead. The war dead.

"There, in the small garden beyond the great oak," the reverend pointed. "That small mausoleum. The garden was the preserve of a wealthy and benevolent plantation owner. He and I spent many pleasant hours there, sitting on a wrought-iron bench, sipping fine Kentucky bourbon, and discussing the vagaries of our all too-fleeting life."

"I reckon you don't have time for that no more," Boone said. "Not with the war that's come."

The reverend shook his head. "No, I don't speak to him anymore. Except in my prayers. He was a precious man to me, wise beyond his years. And sadly, taken from us long before his rightful three score and ten."

"Was it the fightin'?" Boone asked. "Did he go off to the war?"

"No, Boone. The war came to him. And to his family. It came

into his very house and devoured them. The mad beast of war, ravenous for blood, drank its fill from the bloodline of that good man's family. And then it raced off, in search of new flesh to rend." The reverend was silent for a moment, and then looked comfortingly at Boone. "I will confess to you, I have questioned the Lord's wisdom ever since he called back that entire family. Not only the father, but the mother and their innocent children, as well."

Boone composed his thoughts before speaking his heart. "From all I've heard and all I've learned, He moves with reason no man can figure. He teaches with scripture no man can cipher. He damns with a fury no man deserves; yet He seeks our love. Nay, He demands it." Boone put his hand on the reverend's arm. "Parson, I can't help believe that He's no more than the sum of all of us. And beggin' your pardon, sir, I have to ask…isn't there a better way for men to believe?"

The reverend's voice grew hushed with doubt. "I don't know, son. If there is another way, I don't know what it is. I can only hope there is the Heaven that we've all agreed to put our faith in."

"That Heaven comes with a terrible Hell," Boone said. "They are like twins."

"As were the firstborn sons of my friend," said the reverend.

Boone was shocked. "Firstborn? What were their names?"

"Virgil and Aaron."

"Those were Mardi's brother's names," Boone said, with panic rising in his voice.

"I know, Boone. They are here, with their family." He gestured just ahead. "In the Jamerson mausoleum."

There, directly in front of Boone, was a small, open-aired temple of the dead. It was of finely feathered white marble with gold-filigreed engraving. It was almost of a piece with Mardi's carriage. At its apex, it bore the golden name *Jamerson*.

"My God," Boone gasped. "This is their tomb."

"Yes, sir," the reverend said. "Now I want you to read the names that are carved into the marble."

Boone's eyes moved across the gold. "Here lieth the family Jamerson," the filigree said to Boone in a whisper of the dead. A whisper that snaked its way into his mind's ear as if he were hearing the tortured voices of the corpses. "Husband and Father

Charles, beloved Wife and Mother Susanna. Sons Aaron, Virgil and Charles Jr. The lovely Daughters, Lucretia, Lilibeth…and Mardi."

Boone cried out, "No! There's a terrible mistake here!" He turned to the reverend. "Mardi ain't in there." He was almost shouting. "The *rest* of 'em is, but not *her*. She escaped! The Yankees killed 'em all, but Mardi hid out. She's alive! The only one left alive."

"She is not alive, Boone."

"Parson, I held her in my arms." Boone's voice softened a bit with the memory of their lovemaking. "She's living flesh and blood. I was inside of her. She held me to her, warm and tight. I'm telling you, she is a living woman. And I love her."

"She is *dead*, Boone. She is at rest with her family."

"No she ain't! She's at Meadow Wood with Jemmy Jem and Reynard. All the coloreds ran away 'cept for those two. They take care of us, Mardi and me. I aim to spend the rest of my life with her."

"That will be a short life, son," the reverend said. "You're wasting away, even now. Have you looked in a mirror? You are sick, Boone. You are possessed of an evil spirit, sent by Beelzebub. And you are in danger of losing your immortal soul if you die in the throes of possession." The reverend's gray eyes bore into Boone. "And you will surely die if this madness continues."

Boone wrenched himself away from the mausoleum and the skull-like man in black. "Ain't none of it true," he said. "She's a gift from Heaven. An angel." He brusquely broke away and walked off, through the field of dead.

"Wait!" the reverend shouted. "Let her prove it to you herself."

Boone stopped in his tracks. He turned from his retreat, back to the reverend. "Just how would she do *that?*" he said with a derisive laugh. "How could she prove to me she ain't alive?"

"Come with me to the church, Boone. I'll only take up ten more minutes of your time. Then you are free to pursue your destiny."

In the vestibule of the church a stack of paint cans sat off in one corner on a drop cloth. "We're having some restoration done," the reverend said as he moved to the cans.

"That ain't nothin' to me," Boone replied.

"It's to fill the bullet holes," the reverend answered back. "A Yankee raiding party went on a rampage about a year ago, looting and killing and raping. They tore through here like hellhounds. They were men, of sorts, but they had become abominable emissaries of Moloch. They even shot up God's holy church. After they finished here, they rode off to the plantations in the countryside to continue their pillage." A mournful sigh escaped the lips of the skull. "I'm only now getting to the damage. And we'll need some of this paint."

Boone was puzzled. "I ain't of no mind to help you paint, Parson. I got to get back to Mardi."

"Take off your shirt, son."

"I told you, I ain't doin' no work."

"I don't need your *help*, boy. I'm trying to save your *soul*. Now do as I say and turn your back to me. I am going to write some words on your flesh."

"What kind of words?"

"God's words," the skull whispered. "Holy scripture, Boone. Something from one of the psalms. The hundred and twenty-first."

"But why?"

"If she can embrace you, if she can hold you in her arms with these words on your back, then I am wrong. If she can touch holy writ, I am mistaken. If she cannot…then Boone, I leave it to you to decide."

Boone relented and began to strip to the waist. "I don't like it," he said, "but I'll do it. For you, Parson, because you knew Mr. Jamerson, and just to prove you wrong."

The reverend opened one of the paint cans as Boone removed his elegant Jamerson clothing. Naked to the waist, he turned his back to the reverend and just then caught sight of his reflection in a mirror across the vestibule. He was startled. It was clear that his body had lost some of its hard muscularity, and his face was drawn and pallid, with dark circles under his eyes. It looked as if he were somehow being diminished. He shook his head, paid his reflection no mind, and said with a strained bravado, "Do your damage, Parson."

The reverend held the paint can at his waist like an artist's palette and dipped his finger into the pure liquid whiteness. He began to write on Boone's back with the paint as his medium:

The Lord is thy keeper
He preserves thee from
ALL EVIL

FORTY-FOUR

In Chattanooga, Jebber had become, like Boone, known to the citizens of the city. His exploit in killing Colonel Daniel Hennesey was the talk of the town. He was greeted and waved at and cheered for by the good people of Chattanooga. The company of men he commanded used Jebber's fame to their every advantage. "This here is Lieutenant Jeb Stubbs," they announced whenever they could. "He's the man what killed that Yankee what was known as the 'Scourge o' the South.' He's our commander, and we're with him!" they would say, especially in the taverns and cathouses of the city.

Jebber, himself, was having a fine time. He was fed and clothed and cared for by the Army of the Confederacy, though there was really nothing for him to do. His company had not once been 'sent into battle. Their sole task was to guard a stretch of waterfront where Chickamauga Creek entered the Tennessee River. Nothing taxed Jebber's brain as there were no decisions required of him. Consequently, he spent his days strutting about in his plumed hat with his fine sword at his side, acknowledging the respect that was now coming to him for the first time in his life. And he loved it.

But at night he thought of Jewel, and he longed to hold her in his arms again. He desperately wanted to show off his military finery to her, and he desperately wanted to make love to her. But of course he couldn't just up and leave, for there was a war being waged. A war that Jebber didn't really understand, except for the part about the colored's wanting their freedom, and he couldn't see what was so wrong with that. But now that he was a lieutenant in the cavalry, he would have to wait out the war's end before he could return to Jewel and their homestead in Coker Creek Hollow. More and more, with each passing day, he hoped that would be soon.

Now, because Jebber was young and strong and fit as a bull, he found it necessary to avail himself of a working girl from time to time. He found he had to release his pent-up fluids, for they caused a great tension in him, demanding to be freed from the confines of his body. Yet Jebber never thought he was being unfaithful to Jewel, because in his arms, every girl he lay with would become Jewel. He would even call out her name at his moment of climax, and for that brief instant, Jebber always felt as if he were making love to his wife in their cabin in Coker Creek Hollow. He loved his Jewel with every strand of his being.

One night when the sap had risen again, Jebber went out with half a dozen of his men for some evening sport at one of their favorite local establishments. The seven warriors, all wearing their grays, burst loudly through the doors of the Dancing Dog and began to deliver their customary announcement. "Good evening, ladies," one of them said. "We are here with Lieutenant Jeb Stubbs. That famous defender of y'all, for he killed the barbarous Yankee colonel known as the 'Scourge o' the South.' For those of you who never met that damned Yankee, his standing orders to his men exhorted them to defile every Southern woman they met up with. But that devil don't give them orders no more, for Lieutenant Stubbs here slew the bastard in battle with his own bare hands!" The men, then, as if on cue, cheered and shouted for Jebber, raising a rousing huzzah from all the patrons. Jebber, in turn, removed his plumed hat and waved it about, receiving their reception with a gracious bow.

A table was made ready for the warriors, set with glasses, bottles of bourbon and rye, and a platter of pickled eggs and salted meats to slake their appetites. The men took their places and laughed and drank and ate heartily. The piano player knocked out some rags of the day and a few of the men jumped up to dance with the ladies of the evening. Other working beauties came to the table, full of coquettish wiles, and cooed over Jebber's warriors. Everyone was having a fine time, except for Jebber. Things just didn't seem right for him that night. He simply couldn't bring himself to enter into the spirit of the evening, for his thoughts were on Jewel, and how much he missed her. Tonight, no play-acting Jewel would be able to erase the image of her in his mind.

The proprietress of the establishment, one Nellie Pechaud, noticed Jebber's sullen mood and slumped posture and quickly read his distress. After all, it was her calling in life to understand the incompleteness of men. She sashayed across the raucous room, came up behind Jebber, and put both hands on his shoulders. "Why you no happy tonight, Mister Loutenan'?" Nellie asked in her Creole accent. "All is good here at da Dog, don'cha tink?"

Jebber looked up at the rouged and painted woman-of-a-certain-age standing over him. "Oh, yes, ma'am. Everything is right fine."

"So why you no dance or sometin'?" Nellie asked. "You no got no smile on you face. You don't like my girls?"

"It's not that, Nellie. They's all friendly girls. I just miss my Jewel somethin' fierce."

"I bet she young and sweet, eh Mister Loutenan' man? She your wife, no?"

Jebber nodded. "Yep. An' we only been married fer six months afore Boone and me left for big city."

"How long you been gone from her"

"I don't rightly know, Nellie. So much has happened that I plumb done lost track o' time. All's I know is I miss her."

Nellie began to stroke Jebber's hair, like a mother comforting her child. "She gonna be so proud 'a you. When she see you in that *belle chapeau* and you *très bon* uniform. She gonna say, 'My man is a hero.' An' she gonna love you fo' dat."

Jebber felt tears welling up. "That's all I want, Nellie. I just want her to be proud 'a me."

"She gonna be. When 'dis damn war is ovah. But I tell you true, Loutenan', I gonna miss you boys. An' I gonna miss my girls." She continued to run her fingers through Jebber's hair, lovingly. "Ain't gonna be no need for so many girls after da war. So I save my money now. 'Den I gonna go far way, maybe to *Martinique* in da islands. I gonna do nothin' but lay on da beach and let strong, handsome boys like you make Nellie happy. Is a good plan, no?"

"I reckon, Nellie," Jebber said. "But what's Martineek?"

"It's like your Jewel, Loutenan'. It's a long, long way from here." Nellie patted Jebber on the hand. "You never mind. All you need to do is have a good time tonight and forget everyting from da past." She spoke softly into his ear, and her voice took on a soothing, almost hypnotic quality. " 'Dere is only tonight, Loutenan'. Only tonight for you. Noting before...noting to come. Just tonight, like for everyone. Just right here where you are. No place else. Noting more." She stroked his hand in rhythm to her words as Jebber fell under her spell. "Just tonight, Loutenan'. Noting else even exist. Right here, right now. 'Dis is everyting. All for you. For you happiness."

The room swirled around Jebber. Music and laughter and dancing and drinking and life, raging in a desperate time. A time when everyone seemed to fall into the present, forgetting all the things that had come before, and not daring to think of the horrors yet to come.

"Now I want you to come wit' me, Loutenan'," Nellie said. "I got someting special for you upstairs. A new girl. She just come in yesterday. She not like 'dose girls on da dance floor shakin' dey bottoms and tops for anybody dat want 'em. 'Dis one is a good girl. Someting must have happen to her, 'cause she shouldn' even be here doin' what she doin'. But she here. An' 'dis is d' only night dat has ever existed. 'Dis night is for you and for her. You gonna forget all else."

She kissed Jebber on the cheek and took his hand, helping raise him to his feet. They moved through the crowd to cheers and congratulations. Jebber waved his plumed hat and did his best to smile in return, though his heart was not in it. Being a hero of war had lost its novelty for him. All he really wanted was to be back in Coker Creek Hollow. And that was impossible. So he allowed Nellie to lead him across the dance floor of the Dancing Dog to the stairs that led to the second-floor bedrooms.

They climbed the rickety steps as Nellie held tightly to Jebber's hand. "You gonna be happy tonight, Loutenan'," she said. " 'Dis is a nice girl for you. Fresh and young." They walked down a corridor of doors, and then Nellie stopped outside one of them. " 'Dis is it," she said as the music and laughter seemed to fade back into another dimension, leaving Jebber in a kind of limbo where nothing felt of any actual substance. His simple mind had been taken from him by Nellie's words and he was going to do whatever she commanded.

"She's in here, Loutenan'. You wait one second while I make her ready." Nellie knocked on the door and opened it a crack. She poked her head inside and said sweetly, "I got someone for you, *ma petite fleur*. I got you first man, an' he's a hero! He a hansome loutenan', an' he save all da' women of da' South from a terrible Yankee. An' he very lonely for his wife, an' I want you to love him like *you* was his wife. You do dat, no? *Très bon.* Now use some 'a 'dat *eau de toilette* I give you and I gonna send him in."

Nellie closed the door and turned to Jebber. "Now you be good to 'dis girl. Don' do noting rough or mean wit' her. She a little flower and she gonna love you good."

"I won't hurt her," Jebber said. "I would never hurt no girl."

"I know 'dat true," Nellie said. "But I have to say 'dat because 'dis her first time here. I want her happy so she not try to run away."

Jebber reached in his pocket. "How much does she cost, Nellie?"

"You pay me when you finished." Nellie smiled and raised an eyebrow. "What you tink she worth." She stepped back from the door. "Now don't tink about tings. Just go in an' love her." Then she turned away from Jebber and sashayed down the corridor, back to the laughter below.

Jebber stood in front of the door, hesitant yet excited. He swallowed hard, rapped on the door, and said, "I'm comin' in, ma'am."

He opened the door and stepped into a candlelit, perfumed room. And there, sitting shyly on the bed, covered only by a sheer red-silk robe that glistened in the flickering light, was not a substitute, not a figure from his imagination, but Jebber's true wife, Jewel.

FORTY-FIVE

Boone rode with a frenzy through the town of La Fayette and out into the countryside, racing madly back to Mardi. He whipped at the dappled roan and galloped through the lush Georgia vegetation with a fear in his eyes that made him oblivious to everything around him. The child's coffin of silk and gold coins was securely attached to the saddle, but Boone gave it—nor how he would send it to Tennessee—not a thought. His mind held only one image, and that was of Mardi.

As the wind rushed past his face, his time with Mardi flashed as pictures in a book: their lovemaking and laughter, their dining together, the long walks through Meadow Wood, and their delight in each other's company. As the whistling air dried his eyes, he saw Mardi's body in her soft and ruffled finery, pure and innocent, and he longed to hold her again. And then he saw her naked, and knew she was not as the reverend had said. He knew her flesh, and it was smooth and warm with the life of blood coursing through it. He had felt her heart beating in her chest, beating with ecstasy as he had taken her as a woman. His woman.

The minister was simply wrong, Boone thought. Or worse, the minister had been driven mad by the horrors of the war. That was it, Boone reassured himself. The minister, surrounded by the dead, overwhelmed by the dead, had been driven insane. The poor man now saw the dead everywhere, even amongst the living. Why, the parson himself even looked like a corpse. Surely, that was it. And with that knowledge, the knowledge of the reverend's madness, Boone clung to his belief in Mardi and their life together.

All the same, Boone whipped his mount, for he could still not get to Mardi fast enough. Finally, he came to the grand *allée* of oaks with their Spanish moss hanging from their limbs like the tendrils of some unknown sea creature. He slowed the roan's pace as he entered the great green corridor. There now seemed no reason to rush, for he was home. The white columns of the plantation house were at the end of the *allée,* and the sight of them brought a great calm to Boone. His frenzy dissolved into a blue tranquility and he knew he would soon hold his beloved again. He knew Mardi would be in his arms, and he would lose himself in her lovely blue eyes and kiss her golden tresses, her button nose, her flushed cheeks, and delicious red lips. He would take her again, and they would be together forever.

The air beneath the oaks caught a chill as the day turned toward twilight. And Boone became aware of a strange uneasiness in the atmosphere that he had never before felt at Meadow Wood, as if the trees themselves were apprehensive about his return. Long tails of Spanish moss clutched at his clothes, as if trying to hold him back from his rendezvous with Mardi. As if they knew a secret that Boone was not to uncover.

Boone shook his head to clear it of such thoughts. There was no need for disturbing notions rushing about in his mind. He felt discomforted enough with the painted words on his back and the ridiculous story the reverend had spun for him. He certainly didn't want any more troubled imaginings. But the eerie atmosphere under the trees remained, and the sun was dropping fast in its arc—moving into twilight, the time between day and night—the time of transition when the world was neither dark nor light. The time when there was nothing to hold to, when all realities were possible.

And then he saw her. Mardi was rushing down the broad steps of the manor house and calling to him, waving her arms in the air. "Boone! Boone!"

Boone's heart leapt with delight and he waved back to her. "Mardi...I'm here!" He kicked his heels into the roan's ribs and rushed his mount out of the *allée* of whispering trees and onto the cobblestone driveway that ran at the foot of the stairway.

Mardi was a vision in white and she was beaming with all the light of the setting sun. "Boone, my darling," she cried. "I thought I would never see you again."

"I told you I'd be back before sundown," Boone said as he guided his horse to her. Before he could dismount, Mardi hurried to him and embraced his leg.

"My love," she said. "I was so worried. I imagined so many terrible things happening to you." She pressed her cheek to his calf and held tightly to him. "I didn't know what might have happened, or what people might have been saying to you. I didn't want you believing any crazy stories from gossiping town folk." She kissed his calf, rubbing and squeezing it, Boone's foot still in the stirrup.

"Nobody told me nothin', Mardi. They just knew my name, that's all." And he touched her golden hair and bent down from his mount to kiss the top of her head. Her hair was soft and fine in his mouth and again Boone smelled lilacs in the air.

When Mardi felt Boone's lips on her hair she turned up to him and gently kissed his mouth, whispering, "I love you, Boone."

Boone met her kiss and moved his tongue over her teeth and into her mouth. Mardi's tongue came to life with Boone's touch and fluttered with a barely contained passion. Boone wanted her more than he had ever wanted anything in his life. And he also knew that the minister was wrong, for there they were, kissing, in the dim but warming light.

Boone pulled back from their kiss and said, "Step back a bit, Mardi, and let me down off this horse. I want to hold you in my arms."

She smiled and did as Boone asked. In the long rays of the setting sun, Mardi's white dress held a golden burnish. Boone could not believe how beautiful, how radiant she was, standing there before him, glowing in God's holy light. She was like an angel to him. A golden angel. "I do love you, Mardi." He swung his leg over the dappled back of the roan, pirouetted in the stirrup, and jumped gracefully to the ground. He held his arms open to Mardi and she rushed into them, saying only, "Boone," in the bell-like voice of an angel. They wrapped their arms around each other with all the passion of their beings.

Then Mardi screamed! The shriek of a banshee. She tried to pull back from Boone, but he held tight to her. She screamed again and again. "Let me go! You're burning me," she shrieked. "What have you done, Boone?" But he would not let her go. She thrashed her arms against him, flailing wildly and screaming her anguish. "I am burning up. Let me go!"

Her eyes had gone mad with frenzy, a look unlike anything Boone had ever seen before. He was helpless with fear. "Just hold me, Mardi," he said to the banshee in his arms. "Just put your arms around me."

Jemmy Jem and Reynard came rushing out of the Jamerson manor house. "What's wrong down there?" Jemmy shouted. "Is he hurting you, Miss Mardi?"

"I cannot touch you," Mardi wailed at Boone. "Please, let me go!"

"Why, Mardi? Why can't you hold me?"

Mardi screamed in anguish again. "You have betrayed me!"

Boone looked into the face of the writhing thing in his arms—this shrieking creature that had once been his Mardi—and he saw something forbidden, something unholy in her pained features.

"What are you?" he said as he opened his arms and unleashed Mardi from his grasp. She fell back from him and stumbled to the ground, shaking and twisting, like a snake coiling in on itself.

"You have betrayed me," she said in a voice that was crazed and wild. A voice that seemed not to be hers at all.

Jemmy Jem and Reynard rushed up to them as Boone asked again, "What *are* you?"

"What have you done to her?" Jemmy screamed at Boone. "What have you done to my poor baby?"

Boone was blank with shock. He could only stare at Mardi, sprawled on the cobblestones, bent and twisted in an agony that had distorted her sweet features into a hideous mask.

Jemmy knelt down to her mistress and stroked her hair, which was now matted and wet with sweat. "There, there, child," she said. And Mardi, or the thing that had once been Mardi, began to weep great sobs of anguish. They spilled from her in a torrent and Boone was moved to his depths by her pain.

"I didn't mean to hurt her," he said to Jemmy.

Jemmy looked up at him with anger in her eyes. "You *have* hurt her!" she said. "She loved you so very much. She trusted you."

"It wasn't my fault, I swear," Boone said. "That reverend, he wrote words on me."

Reynard bent down and lifted up Mardi in his arms. "I'll take her inside now," he said to Jemmy. And he began to carry her off to the Jamerson manor house. The grand house of the family of which Mardi was the sole survivor. The last of the line.

Jemmy watched her mistress being carried away, and then turned on Boone. "What words?"

"I don't know, Jemmy. He said somethin' from scripture. And he put it on my back."

"The parson in town?" Jemmy asked.

Boone nodded. "He showed me where they's all buried."

"They ain't all there," Jemmy said.

"I seen the crypt, Jemmy. It says all the names. Mardi's name is there."

"She ain't there, you fool. Reynard is carryin' her up the stairs right now! Look fer yerself."

Boone turned to watch as Reynard rose up the steps with Mardi cradled in his arms. They passed through the great oak doors and disappeared into the gloom within the mansion.

"What's he carryin' if that ain't Miss Mardi?" Jemmy asked Boone.

"I don't know," Boone said. "The parson told me if she couldn't touch me..." Boone shuddered with the thought. "Then she was dead."

"She ain't dead! You made love to her." Jemmy's voice was imploring. "Did you make love to something that was cold and dead? No! You made love to a warm, living woman."

"That was before the words," Boone said.

"Show me them words," Jemmy brusquely demanded.

Boone began to take off his jacket just as the first drop of rain fell. They both looked up into the sky and saw a black thunderhead rolling in from the north. A mean wind had come up, pushing the piled clouds over Meadow Wood and bringing a dank chill to the air.

"Come inside, Mister Boone," Jemmy said. "It looks like a nasty night is rearin' up its head. We got a fire goin' in the library." Jemmy's voice had returned to its warm, motherly tone. "I wouldn't want you to catch nothin' takin' your shirt off out here. You kin show me what that reverend wrote when we's by the fire. An' then I wants to tell you a story that's gonna make you see things in a whole different way."

She took Boone's hand and led him to the manor house. A flash of lightning crackled from the clouds, spiking down to earth and striking one of the giant gnarled oaks of the *allée*. Thunder boomed as the great oak split with a terrible creak, and then fell dead to the earth.

"God's angry tonight, Jemmy," Boone said. "Powerful angry."

"No he ain't, Mister Boone. That's nature at work. God don't care one way or the other."

The rain fell hard and Jemmy and Boone, hand in hand, raced for the shelter of the Jamerson mansion. Boone looked up one last time, through the ominous, black clouds, and glimpsed the pale glow of a full moon.

FORTY-SIX

"Jewel?" Jebber said to the red-silk-wrapped figure on the bed. "Is that you?" He almost couldn't be sure in the dance of the flickering candlelight. But in his heart he knew it was Jewel.

Jewel recognized him as soon as he had set foot in the room. "It's me, Jebber," she said in an embarrassed voice.

"You're the new gal?"

"I am, Jebber. I just got here late last night."

Jebber closed the door behind him. "But what're you doin' here? Why ain't you home?"

"I can't be home," she said. "I ain't no good no more."

"Jewel, what're you talkin' about? Of course yer good!" Jebber approached the bed, laying his plumed hat on a chair.

"I ain't, Jebber. I'm ruined."

"You don't look ruined to me," he said.

"Inside, I am."

"Are you sick?"

"No, Jebber. I ain't sick."

"You didn't have to be cut by no doctor, did you?" Jebber asked with sudden worry. Jewel just shook her head, afraid to tell any more.

He stood now at the foot of the bed, looking at her, realizing how much he loved her and how beautiful she was. "God, you are beautiful, Jewel." He paused to stare at her, and Jewel's heart filled with shame. "You don't look ruined no how. An' if you ain't been to the cuttin' doctor and you ain't sick, why ain't you home?"

"It's my soul, Jebber." She hung her head. "It's gone. They took my soul."

Jebber became even more confused. "Jewel, can't nobody take yer soul. Only God kin do that. An' you is alive and well, so's you must still have it. You only lose it when yer dead."

She looked up at him, tears in her eyes. "I ain't no good for you anymore, Jebber. Don't you understand? I'm a whore!"

"So what?" he said. "That happens to lots 'a girls durin' wartime. Why, there's workin' girls all over Chattanooga, an' they's all nice people. They ain't ruined, an' you ain't neither. Yer the most beautiful thing in the world to me, Jewel."

"But ain't you ashamed of me?" she asked.

"How could I be? Yer my wife."

She buried her face in her hands. "Yankees come to the farm, Jebber," she said through her tears, confessing the terrible anguish in her heart. "They raped me."

Jebber sat down next to Jewel and comfortingly stroked her hair. "Don't you pay that no mind, darlin'. But I swear to God, if we ever find them, I will kill them all." Jewel sobbed with shame as Jebber continued to stroke her hair. "You just forget about it now, Jewel, you hear me? Things happen in war, an' you just got to let 'em go." He kissed her on the top of her head and she smelled like flowers to him. "I love you, Jewel, and as long as yer alive, nothin' else matters to me."

"Oh, Jebber," Jewel said as she wrapped her arms around her man. She hugged him tightly, clinging to him as if he held her soul within him; as if by holding him to her she might be able to retrieve her lost spirit from his body, reclaiming it as her own.

And so they sat, clinging to one another on the side of the bed in the little, candlelit room, upstairs at the Dancing Dog. And little by little, Jebber's warmth and his great love for his wife began to fill the void in Jewel's heart, and she was made whole again.

"My God, Jebber," she said, smiling, "I think you have given me my soul back." She squeezed him with all her might. "I feel so good inside. I feel all warm and safe in your arms."

"That's what I'm here for, Jewel," Jebber softly said. "I am yer man an' I will always love you."

Jewel eased back from him, laughing with a newfound joy. "Well then, Mister Stubbs, suppose you just love me right now." She let her red-silk robe fall from her shoulders. "For I am surely your woman this night."

Jebber could only stare at the naked figure before him, as beautiful as a goddess, her arms held out to him. "Make love to me," she said. "Make me think nothing has happened, and nobody is dead, and you never went away. Just love me, Jebber."

Jebber stood up from the bed. "Jewel, you are so beautiful. Let me take my uniform off an' then I'm gonna…"

"How on earth did you *get* that uniform, Jebber? You didn't steal it, did you?"

"Heck no! They gave me it. I'm a lootenant in the Confederate Army. An' I'm a hero." He went to the chair, took up his hat, and set it on his head. "Look at me, Jewel. Don't I look like a hero?" He turned a slow circle to show himself off. "Ain't this a grand uniform? And ain't this hat the prettiest thing you ever did see?"

Jewel giggled. "It surely is, darlin'. But I really think it belongs more on a woman's head than a man's, what with those feathers and all."

"Jewel!" Jebber said, putting his hands on his hips. "Them feathers is what makes this hat special."

Jewel giggled again. "Jebber, it looks like the kind of hat to be worn by one of those men that…well, you know…likes other men."

Jebber couldn't believe his ears. "You mean like a sissy man?"

"I'm afraid so, darlin'."

Jebber drew his saber, the engraved blade that once belonged to Colonel Daniel Hennesey. "Well jest give a look-see at *this*, Jewel. This didn't belong to no sissy man. This belonged to the 'Scourge o' the South.' I took it from him." The saber glistened in the candlelight. Jebber ripped a few wild thrusts and swipes through the air as if he were cutting off the heads of Yankee devils.

Jewel put her hands to her mouth and sat straight up. "Jebber, you didn't kill no one, did you?"

Jebber stopped lopping off heads and held the sword aloft like a torch. "I'm a hero, Jewel."

"I know that, darlin'. And you *look* like a hero. But did you *kill* anyone?"

Jebber brought the saber to his side and slowly put it back

in its scabbard. He hung his head, unable to meet Jewel's eyes. "No, I didn't, Jewel. All's I did was take the sword from some dead body and Boone made up a story sayin' I killed a bunch 'a Yankees so's the Rebs wouldn't hang us for bein' spies."

"*Hang* you?" Jewel cried in shock. "*Spies?* What in heaven's name did you two get into? And where's Boone?"

"I don't know, Jewel. Sellin' his wares, I reckon. That's why we came in the first place."

"Oh, Jebber," Jewel said in exasperation. She held her arms out once again to him. "Just come to bed, will you?"

Jebber gave her his best smile. "But don't you think I look grand?"

"Yes, darlin'," she said. "You do look grand, and you *are* my hero."

Jebber whooped, "Hoo-whee! That's all I wanted to hear."

FORTY-SEVEN

Boone and Jemmy Jem stood before the fireplace in the Jamerson library, warming themselves by the hardwood logs and popping embers of the crackling blaze. Outside, the rain fell cold and angry on the roof and windowpanes of the great manor house. Upstairs, echoing through the empty rooms, Boone could hear screams and anguished shrieks from the betrayed Mardi.

"What is she, Jemmy?" Boone asked.

"You held her in your arms, Mister Boone. You made love to her." Jemmy smiled at him. "Ain't she everythin' you want in a woman?"

"Not if she's *dead*."

"She ain't dead," Jemmy said.

Boone slipped out of his coat. "The parson at the cemetery where the family's buried said she is." He let his coat fall to the floor, stripped off his shirt, then turned his back to Jemmy. "Here's the words he wrote on me. An' just like he said, she couldn't hold me."

Jemmy looked at Boone's now emaciated back and read aloud the words of the psalm. *"The Lord is thy keeper,"* she said haltingly. *"He preserves thee from all evil."*

Boone nodded. "That's what he said he wrote."

Jemmy shook her head. "Why, Mister Boone? Why did you do it? You was so happy with her."

Boone put his shirt and coat back on as he spoke sternly to Jemmy. "Tell me the truth. What is she?"

Jemmy turned away from Boone and looked into the fire. She began to hum softly to herself, some lullaby that sounded not of the New World, but of some ancient African kingdom. Her eyes began to roll back in her head, exposing the whites as she slipped off into a trance. She spoke in a deep, husky voice—a disembodied tone that came from someone who was not Jemmy Jem.

"I have always existed between two worlds," the voice rising from within Jemmy said. "Of black skin, and of white. Amid earthbound beings and the realm of the invisible." The flames curled amidst the logs in the hearth and leapt enticingly, as if they had joined Jemmy's words in a sympathetic rhythm. "From the day of Mardi's birth, I fed her life from the milk of my breasts. I nurtured that child, and taught her about life and its mysteries. She understood things. More than the other Jamerson children, she was a child of nature. She loved the green of the woods. She loved to lose herself in the forest. And the lake, my Lord, how she loved the waters of the lake."

Jemmy turned to look at Boone, her eyes once again soft and brown, the eyes of compassion and comfort that Boone had grown to love. "And she loved the night, Mister Boone. She was *my* child more than a Jamerson. We shared an understanding that was beyond words. It was as if our souls had come from the same place. I am of the *Yoruba* people in Africa. I am an American colored woman, but my heart, my spirit, my soul are of the *Yoruba*. Sometimes, I think Miss Mardi is of the *Yoruba*, too. Sometimes I think she is the soul of a princess come to join me in the New World. And sometimes I think we were sisters in an ancient time. I believe she was to be the queen one day, and I was a woman of the plants and herbs. A healing woman, a shaman. Even as I am today, Mister Boone. And I am with the soul of my sister. She is my white child and I am her black nanny, but we are both creatures of the forest."

She took Boone's hand in hers, and her eyes were imploring. "Her happiness means everything to me, Mister Boone. I know that it does to you, too. I can see it in your eyes. Stay with her. Love her, as in your heart you know you do. She is your woman. You know that is true."

Boone pulled his hands from Jemmy's grip. "She is dead, Jemmy. And you brought her back to life, didn't you? That's what you did."

Jemmy nodded. "Yes, Mister Boone. She lives because of me."

"How is such a thing possible? How can you bring a dead

thing back to life?"

Jemmy gazed into the twisting flames, and when she spoke, again they danced in rhythm to her words. "It's not so hard, Mister Boone. There are herbs and potions. There are rites and chants. It's just a matter of knowing…and believing. In this part of the New World, here in the South, many things are possible. Do you know the word, *voodou*, Mister Boone? Do you know what comes to us from the Caribbean, from the island of Haiti? Do you know of the *dupys* from Jamaica?"

The fire crackled with a new intensity, as if the flames were enlivened by these words that Jemmy—or the voice in Jemmy—was speaking into the heated air.

"Do you know of Baron Samedi in New Orleans, and of Marie Laveau? You see, many things—including the rites of my *Yoruba* people, and also the magic of the *Dogon* tribe of Africa—come together here in the South." Jemmy looked at Boone. "Anything is possible, Mister Boone. But only if you have love in your heart."

"You took her body from the crypt, didn't you? She isn't there at all!"

Jemmy nodded. "That's right, Mister Boone."

"In the name of God, why?"

"For *love*," Jemmy said. "For her to know the love between a man and a woman. You see, Mardi was torn from this world before ever knowing the pleasures of the flesh. She was stolen from life by those Yankees who came into our house. And she never knew why God created us male and female. She never knew the great joy of love, of lying in a man's arms, of holding a man inside of her. I wanted her to feel that burning love of youth. I wanted her to know the flames and the heat of that passion. But she was taken too young. She is only seventeen, Mister Boone."

"My God, she's just a child," Boone said.

"No, she is a woman now," Jemmy said. "Because of *you*, my sweet Mister Boone. You are the man who has completed her. *You* have made her a woman." A shriek came from the room upstairs, a terrible cry of anguish, echoing through the Jamerson manor house. Jemmy looked up to the ceiling of the library. "She cries out for the love of you, Mister Boone. She wants you with her, always." The voice that was inside of Jemmy grew soft and mesmerizing. "Stay with her. Stay here at Meadow Wood. Stay here for the rest of your life, Mister Boone. She loves you, and she will always love you. You know that, and you know that you love *her*, too. She is your woman. Love her, Mister Boone. Love her here, at Meadow Wood. Forever."

Jemmy withdrew a knotted bandana from the folds of her skirt. She untied the gingham cloth, revealing its contents: a handful of rich, dark soil. The loamy earth of Meadow Wood plantation. The fertile earth of Georgia, of the New World. With a wave of her free arm, she drew a crossroads in the air. Then she moved the cloth and the soil through the center of the cross, plunging it back and forth. Her voice rose with a gripping intensity as she recited an incantation:

"From the powers of life
From the powers of the earth,
From the love of all things,
To the love of this man.
I ask you, Ogun, I pray you, Shango
I beseech you Legba, I implore you Azaka
I beg you Masa
And I command you all!
Let this man stay here.
Forever!"

The fire roared and cracked like rifle shot. Flames leapt high with a life of their own, as if animated from within, taken over by some entity at the heart of the blaze. The flames swayed in time with Jemmy's words:

"To all whose names are remembered,
To all whose names are lost.
I offer up a place,
To stand upon this earth.
To all who came before,
To all who will come after,
I give you life…and love…and laughter.
And I command you all!
Let this man stay here.
Forever!"

Jemmy's fingers dug soil from the bandana and she scattered it through the matrix of the imaginary crossroads, into the fire. An explosive rush swept the hearth as the flames fed hungrily at the earth. As if they wanted to devour anything and everything that came near them, even the source of life itself.

"No!" Boone cried out. "I cannot. I already have a wife. We have two children. I must go home to them."

Jemmy's eyes flashed with hatred at this revelation. "You never said anything *before!* You never *told us!* Why?"

Boone stammered, "I...I don't know. The war maybe?"

Jemmy howled with rage and hurled the bandana and remaining dirt into the fireplace. "You can go home to the *devil*, Boone Dillard!"

The flames roared with appreciation at her gift. They leapt and danced around the gingham, quickly consuming the cloth, only to soar higher, filling the cavernous hearth of the Jamerson library with a terrible heat. Suddenly, the harpsichord began to play. It was an insane melody of cacophony and rage, propelled by a pounding and slamming of the keys. Boone held his hands to his ears, trembling with fear. Then, amidst the inferno in the fireplace, Mardi's image began to form. She took shape, and then slowly stepped forth from the blaze, flames licking the hem of her dress.

The storm outside shot a flash of lightning over the Jamerson manor house and the room was awash with sickly blue daylight for that instant. A concussive clap of thunder followed immediately, shaking the mansion to its very foundation. Boone stood transfixed with fear and disbelief.

The figure from the fireplace held her arms out to Boone, and it *was* Mardi. "My darling," she said. "Come to me."

Boone found himself unable to move. The strength had gone out of his limbs, his will entirely drained by the unearthly presence that stood before him. And yet it was Mardi. And he knew he loved her.

"Please, Boone," Mardi said. "I must keep you. You are my man. You are everything to me. Without you I cannot live." Her soft blue eyes bore into Boone's and he felt himself falling into them. She looked just as she did when he first saw her, when her beauty first took his breath away. She was draped in crenulated white, her golden hair cascading loosely over her delicate shoulders. Her lips were full and red, and she smiled at him with a tenderness that began to melt his heart.

Boone didn't know what to believe anymore. There she stood before him, more beautiful than ever. How could she not be alive? How could something so lovely, so sweet and imploring be a dead thing? It made no sense to Boone. The minister, he thought, *must* be wrong.

"Mardi," Boone said, "the parson said you were dead. That you died with your family at the hands of those Yankees. But you are here, before me, more beautiful than ever. How?"

Mardi smiled with all her sweetness. "Hush, Boone," she said as she put a finger to his lips. "Don't believe anything but what you hold in your heart. I am here for you, as I always will be. Now, take me in your arms."

"But you couldn't hold me," he said. "You couldn't touch the words of scripture."

She smiled again and opened her arms. "Boone, I love you. Let us wed and live together…in eternal love."

Boone, unable to resist her, stepped into her arms and Mardi coiled his body with her embrace. She pressed her lips to his mouth with an all-consuming need. Boone returned her kiss and wrapped his arms around her.

The flames of the fire stretched upward with delight and crackled furiously. Jemmy hissed at the embraced pair, "How dare you betray her, Boone Dillard." Jemmy reached into the pocket of her skirt, took out a small *gris-gris* bag and flung it into the fire. "Try to go home, now!"

As Mardi and Boone kissed, locked in embrace, Boone's clothes began to catch fire. Where Mardi's hands touched the coat on his back—at the very place covering the words of scripture written by the minister—the cloth began to burn. Boone's eyes went wide with terror. He jerked frantically out of Mardi's hold, but in an instant, the entire back of his garment was ablaze. He screamed and ran toward a large picture window at the far end of the room, rain whipping outside at the pane.

Mardi called insanely to him. "Boone! Stay with me."

Boone tore at the casement, struggling to open the window, his coat now a torrent of fire. In his wild thrashing, the flowing floor-to-ceiling draperies caught the fire from his garment and burst into flames. Jemmy Jem laughed maniacally. Mardi screamed out, "Boone! Love me, Boone. Forever!"

With those words echoing in his ears, Boone hurled himself through the broad glass pane, shattering the window in a shower of glass shards. He reeled across the veranda and threw himself onto the wet lawn, rolling over and over in the pounding rain. A jagged bolt of lightning streaked the sky and exploded on the Jamerson mansion. A dazzling glare of ice-blue light flared up. Boone scrambled across the lawn on his hands and knees, seeking the shelter of the *allée*.

When he reached the first great oak he turned back to the mansion and saw it was engulfed in flames. Ablaze from the fire within and the lightning bolt from without, the Jamerson home was being consumed by fiery shafts of red and orange and yellow. It was as if the fire in the hearth of the library had called forth the lightening from the heavens and they were insanely devouring everything. Boone stared in shock at the conflagration, his mind tumbling with images of Mardi. His energy began to slip away and he felt himself growing faint. Then, through the shattered window of the library, he saw a figure in white, her arms outstretched, engulfed by the consuming flames. He knew it was Mardi, and as she disappeared into the fiery holocaust, he thought he could hear her words: "Boone, I'm waiting for you, Boone. I'm waiting for you."

With his consciousness slipping away and a blackness overcoming him, Boone turned from the horror of the burning mansion and looked up into the storm-racked sky. The thunderheads parted briefly, revealing a glimpse of the full moon through sheets of pouring rain. He stared skyward as his consciousness slipped away; and the last image his mind registered was of two thin clouds encircling the full, shimmering orb, wrapping themselves around it, like the arms of a woman. And just as Boone blacked out, he realized it was a snake moon.

FORTY-EIGHT

Upstairs at the Dancing Dog, Jebber awoke in the arms of his beloved Jewel. For an instant, he thought he was back home in the warm, rumpled bed of their little cabin in Coker Creek Hollow. Then he heard the music and singing from downstairs and he knew where he was. It was one o'clock in the morning and he was at Nellie Pechaud's, in the arms of the new girl.

Jebber's mind became clear as a great purpose came over him. "Wake up, Jewel. We're goin' home." He kissed his wife gently on the forehead. "Come on, darlin'. Wake up now."

Jewel stirred and wrapped her arms around Jebber's neck. She kissed him full on the mouth and Jebber could feel the happiness in her kiss. "I love you, Jebber," she said as she took her lips from his. "You are the world to me."

"Come on, honey. We got to put our clothes on. We're goin' home!" He smiled at her and hopped out of bed, and in the flickering candlelight, Jewel thought that the naked man reaching his hand out to her was the most beautiful thing she had ever seen. She took his hand and Jebber gave her a quick tug that made her almost fly up to her feet.

"Jebber!" Jewel squealed. "You are just about the strongest and most handsome man on this here earth." She pressed her body against his and held him tightly. "Now what did you just say about home?"

He gave her a quick squeeze and slapped her bare bottom. "I made up my mind, Jewel. This is all over. For both of us. We're goin' home. Tonight! So get dressed, you hear?" He released her from his powerful arms and began to put on his uniform.

"But you can't just leave the army, Jebber. Can you?"

"Sure I can. I ain't never really belonged in the first place. Not in my heart."

Jewel took down a dress hanging in the room's cramped wardrobe. "But I owe Nellie money. She paid for me."

Jebber faced Jewel as she slipped into the dress. "You mean she bought you? Like a slave?"

"That's about it," Jewel said, ashamed.

Jebber laughed. "Well, you're free now, darlin'. This war is all about freein' the slaves. *All* the slaves." His booming, infectious laugh tickled Jewel, and she realized that with her man, anything was possible.

"You got more clothes than just that dress, ain't you?"

Jewel nodded and took out a small carpetbag from inside the wardrobe. "Everything's in here," she said.

"Now don't forget that fancy robe you was wearin' when I first come in. I want you to wear that on *special* nights when we're home," he said with a sly grin on his face.

Jewel blushed as she put the silk robe into her bag. Jebber buttoned the collar on his uniform, buckled on his sword belt, donned his plumed hat, and bowed to Jewel. "Well, Missus Stubbs, I do believe we are ready to go."

Jewel smiled, took his arm, and they headed out into the music and smoke and whisky stench of the Dancing Dog.

Nellie Pechaud saw them as they came down the stairs. "Where you tink you go?" she said to Jewel from the bottom of the staircase.

"I'm goin' home with my husband," Jewel said as they brushed past Nellie and walked haughtily across the dance floor.

Nellie was hot on their heels. "You go nowhere, lil' miss fancy ting," she said. "You got to work off two hundred dollars. You forget? I own you."

Jebber whirled on her and swiftly withdrew his saber. The saber of the "Scourge of the South." Nellie screamed in fear as Jebber swung the gleaming steel over her head.

"Don' kill me! Don' cut Nellie's head off! Please Mister Loutenan'!"

Jebber laughed and dropped the saber at Nellie's feet. "I reckon this should pay any 'a what my wife owes," he said. Then he took off his plumed hat and tossed it on the floor next to the sword. "An' take this here fancy hat, too. I don't need it no more." Nellie was left speechless as Jebber and Jewel turned away and headed for the door.

A shout crossed the room from the table where Jebber's men sat, drunk as skunks. "Hold on, there, Lieutenant, sir. Just where you goin' to?" The voice came from Jebber's sergeant, Jonathon Ripton.

Jebber stopped and looked over at his men. Then he looked at Jewel. "You go stand by the door, honey. I'll only be a minute." Jewel did as he asked and Jebber walked up to the table of drunks.

"Boys," he said, "I'm goin' home. I done come to my senses and I'm goin' home. An' I might offer y'all do the same, too."

The sergeant spoke up. "That's desertin', sir. They'll hang you fer it."

Jebber drew his side arm and one by one, pointed it at each man at the table. "Not if they don't catch me," he said. Then he trained the gun on Sergeant Ripton. "An' they won't *catch* me if you boys don't say nothin' for a day or so. And they sure as hell ain't never gonna *find* me where I'm goin.'" He pressed the pistol against Ripton's forehead. "So can I have your word on that, Sergeant?"

Ripton stammered as a cold sweat of fear beaded his brow. "Yes...yes, sir, Lieutenant Stubbs."

"That's good, Sergeant." Then Jebber waved the pistol at the other soldiers, who had quickly sobered from their stupor. An' your word, too, boys?"

"Yes, sir. Yes, sir," they said almost in unison.

"Well, I thankee. Y'all are good men," Jebber said as he holstered his sidearm. Then he ripped his lieutenant's bars from the shoulders of his uniform. "Sergeant Ripton," Jebber said as he held out the bars in the palm of his hand, "I am now promotin' you to the lootenant of this here company. I know you'll do a fine job." He turned his hand, dumping the bars on the whisky-wet table.

Ripton grabbed at them greedily. "Thank you, sir," he said. "I'll do my best, sir."

"I know you will, Sergeant," Jebber said. He raised his hand to his forehead in salute: "Goodbye, boys." Then he turned from the table, went to Jewel at the door, took her arm, and said, "Let's go home, sweetheart."

A worried look crossed Jewel's face. "I don't know if it's gonna be as easy as that, Jebber. They said you'd be a deserter."

"Jewel," Jebber said with a big smile on his face. "As long as we love each other, can't nothin' harm us."

"But it's a long way to Coker Creek," Jewel protested. "What if they come after us?"

"Don't you fear fer nothin', darlin'." He kissed his wife lightly on the cheek, swung open the door of the Dancing Dog, and Mister and Missus Jebber Stubbs disappeared into the night.

FORTY-NINE

"*Wake up*, you!" a voice shouted at Boone. He slowly opened his eyes and a flood of light rushed in. The sun was high in the sky and Boone had been in a state of non-existence for many hours. Now, his consciousness gradually came back into his control as he began to regain a grasp of reality. He squinted at the brightness of the sunlight and saw vaguely through his fluttering eyelashes the outline of four men on horseback. They were Confederate soldiers.

"Wake up, there!" the lead man shouted again. "What you doin' 'round here, boy? Lookin' to steal somethin'?" The man prodded at Boone with a long switch from the lightning-split oak. "We *hang* looters, ya'know."

That brought Boone fully awake. He sat up quickly and looked at the soldier—a boy of no more than twenty with two corporal stripes on his sleeve. "I ain't no looter. I was here yesterday with Mardi Jamerson and her servants, Jemmy Jem and Reynard. I'm a guest of the house."

The boy in a man's uniform laughed. "You was a guest yesterday?" The other men joined him in laughter. "You must'a been drinkin' a whole snootful of some mean white lightnin' to come up with *that* crazy story," the boy said.

"Ain't no story," Boone said. "An' I ain't been drinkin'." He rose to his feet and looked across the lawn at the charred remains of the once magnificent plantation house of the Jamerson family. "That burned to the ground last night," he said. "It was struck by the wrath of God. A bolt from the heavens."

The men roared with laughter. "That bolt came outta that white lightnin' bottle, Corporal," one of the men said.

The boy in charge nodded his head. "I reckon as how, Private Peters. Now you go look around, see he ain't looted nothin'."

"Yes, sir," Peters said as he moved his horse off toward the ruins.

The corporal spoke to one of the other horsemen. "Circle about the other way, Clawson. Make sure he ain't done nothin' funny here abouts. I don't take to drunks hangin' around anywheres near my jurisdiction."

Boone shouted at the retreating soldiers, "You boys see if there's any sign of a colored man and woman. See if they's alive."

The corporal prodded Boone hard in the ribs with his switch. "Hey, shut up! I give the orders around here. Don't you be tellin' my men nothin'."

Boone angrily slapped the stick away. "Well then, you tell them, sonny. See if Jemmy and Reynard are still alive."

The boy laughed again. "You fool drunk. There ain't no servants round these ruins."

Boone scowled at the boy. "They was here last night. Before the conflagration. Before God hurled his wrath at the unholiness that was upon this land."

"Last night?"

"That's right. I just told you. It all caught fire with the flames of Hell and burned to the *ground* last night," Boone said.

"You're crazy, mister," the corporal said. "This house burned down a *long* time back. They say the colored nanny set fire to it when all her white people was killed by a raidin' party 'a Yanks." He spat on the ground. "Bastards."

Boone couldn't believe his ears. "But I was in the house last night. I was with Mardi and Jemmy and Reynard. An' then the fire—"

The boy cut him off. "No you *weren't*, mister!" The corporal took a deep breath and surveyed the ruins of the Jamerson plantation. "I should know, 'cause I been patrollin' these parts for the last half year. This place ain't been nothin' but ash and cold ruins since I first come upon it."

All time seemed suspended as the boy's words penetrated Boone's consciousness. The terrible truth began to consume him as emptiness swirled down from his brain to the pit of his stomach. He felt himself falling into a black space, alone and terrified.

Then a shout from one of the soldiers brought him back to a chilling reality. "Corporal, he's a looter!" Private Peters rode up with Boone's horse in tow. The coffin-like box still cinched to the saddle was now pried open. "Look what I found in this here box," Peters said.

The corporal pulled out the bolts of Chinese silk. "Pretty fancy stuff for a drunk," he said. Then he saw the small leather bag, and as he opened it his eyes went wide at the sight of the gold coins. He let out a long whistle. "This here is a powerful lot 'a money. You find this in the ashes, mister?"

"That's my money," Boone said. "Jemmy Jem paid me that for my pottery."

"The colored woman?" the boy said. "And I suppose there's pottery to be found 'neath those ashes?"

"If you'd look," Boone said. "You'd find it."

The boy shook his head. "Mister, I do believe you're tetched. We sure as hell ain't gonna go lookin' in no ashes for the remains 'a nothin'! The only thing in them ashes is *ghosts*." He put the bag of gold coins in his pocket. "Now, I'm confiscatin' these here coins in the name of the Confederate Army and the sovereign state of Georgia. An' I'll be takin' that fancy cloth, too, as per my orders."

"That's for my *wife*," Boone said. "I bought them bolts with some of the money Jemmy paid me. An' that bag of coins is for my boys. That don't belong to the state of Georgia! That's all mine!"

The corporal gave a snort of derision. "Mister," he said, "I ought to hang you right here and now for lootin'. These big ol' oak trees got some fine sturdy branches for takin' a rope. They'd hold you up real nice for a good swingin' with a *noose* around your neck." He leaned over and looked Boone hard in the eyes. "That's what we do with looters, mister."

"I ain't no looter," Boone said.

The corporal sat back up in his saddle, "Maybe you is, and maybe you ain't. But I ain't gonna hang you. 'Cause the sovereign state of Georgia don't allow the hangin' of *crazy* people." The other soldiers laughed as the boy turned his horse. "Now, I suggest you git, mister," the corporal said over his shoulder. " 'Cause if I see you round these parts again, I surely *will* hang you."

He spurred the flanks of his horse and rode off down the *allée* of oaks. His men, each with a bolt of Cassy's silk under an arm, followed close behind.

Boone watched them disappear, and then turned to his horse. He untied the child's coffin from the saddle straps and let it fall to the ground. He swung astride the roan, and before he could turn to ride away from Meadow Wood, a fox darted out of the underbrush, scurried across the lawn, and ran directly into the ashes of the manor house of the Jamerson family.

FIFTY

It took Boone almost two weeks to work his way back to Coker Creek Hollow, and on his journey he saw far too much of the bleakness and the horrors of war. He saw the bodies of men and the carcasses of animals, he saw burning buildings, destroyed towns, ruined farm houses, scorched fields, slaughtered livestock, wasted crops, and he saw weeping women and ragged children. He saw the devastation men were capable of inflicting upon one another. And he understood the insanity that comes over men in time of war—for it had come over both him and Jebber. And for that he was profoundly ashamed.

It was far into the night when he finally came over the rise from the south and looked down into his little valley. There was only a half-moon in the sky, but the night was clear, and the moon cast just enough light for Boone to see his house, Jebber's house, the barn and smokehouse and his little kiln. It was all peaceful and quiet, just as Boone remembered it, and he smiled to himself. Things were just the way they were supposed to be, and he knew now that it was his refuge from the madness of the world and his heart was gladdened.

He moved his horse slowly through the green and down the rise. He was filled with excitement and the anticipation of being in Cassy's arms again, and of seeing his boys once more. Inside, he was leaping with delight, but he rode into the hollow carefully and softly, not wanting to wake anyone in the darkened cabins. He moved past his field, now lush with summer corn, and his mind raced back to planting time when at the barren field's edge he had first seen the white figure. The figure that had called to him from behind the green wall of the forest on the night of the snake moon. He passed Jebber's house and hoped that Jebber had come to his senses and was now fast asleep, wrapped in the arms of his sweet Jewel. But Jebber and Jewel could wait until morning, Cassy and the boys were all that was on his mind.

He passed his kiln, the smokehouse where the pig that Chap had slaughtered was cured, Cassy's chicken coop, and the barn in which the milk cow slept. The thought came to Boone that it was time for more livestock, now that there were two boys who would be growing and hungry. He smiled at the pictures tumbling through his mind of Chap and the baby, grown to teenagers, running and laughing and jumping like fawns gamboling in the light of the sun, in the peace and joy of Coker Creek Hollow.

As he slipped down out of the saddle and reined his horse to a post-rail of his cabin, Boone could see thin, warm light glowing from within. He walked softly across the rickety porch steps, closed his eyes, and spoke with hushed gratitude, "Thank you, Lord," then pushed open the door of his home.

And there, huddled next to the stove in the orange wash of shimmering embers, was his wife, Cassy. Before his footfall could cross the threshold, she immediately turned and said, "Boone! I knew it was you."

"Cassy! My sweet love." She rushed across the room, and fell into his open arms as she smothered him with kisses. They held each other with a desperate passion in a moment of eternity. Time drew itself in and took a deep breath that made all the world stop and rest in the embrace of the two lovers—husband and wife, bonded once more.

Boone's eyes welled with tears of relief and joy. "Oh, my dear, sweet Cassy. How foolish I have been." He stroked her hair as Cassy pressed her body deep into his. He could feel her breasts tight against his chest, so firm and swollen with milk for the baby. Her hips were thrust to his groin, calling to his manhood. The entire length of her body squirmed to touch Boone in every place, in every way that it could.

"I love you so much, Boone," Cassy said as she feverishly kissed at his lips and cheeks and eyes and ears, pressing her mouth over every curve and angle of Boone's face. "I don't care what you've done. You have come back to me, and that's the only thing that matters."

Boone took her mouth to his, his passion and love for his

woman storming inside of him. "My beautiful wife," he said. "Out there, in that world of war and men's desires, I lost myself." His fingers combed through her thick hair as he nestled her head into his shoulder. "Now that you're in my arms again, I realize something had come over me. Some kind of madness."

"Hush, Boone," Cassy whispered to her beloved. "You don't have to tell me these things. I don't need to know any of it. All I need is you in my arms, and for me, the light has been renewed again. I so feared you were dead. I didn't know what had happened to you. All manner of terrible things went through my mind." She looked up into his eyes and smiled with all the radiance of the sun. "The Lord has brought you back to me. To our home and our sons. I know you will never leave me again." She kissed him softly on his cheek. "I will be with you as long as you love me, my dearest Boone."

"Cassy," Boone said as he held her to his heart, "you are my wife. And before God and all the forces of nature I will be your husband, forever." The swirling energy flowing from the core of his heart enfolded Cassy in gold. And they stood there in the cradle of their little home, in Coker Creek Hollow, wrapped in each other's arms. And the earth smiled at two of its children, joined again in love.

The universe revolved around itself, until at last time came back to its proper dimension and Cassy said, "How hungry you must be, my Boone. Do you want to eat something?"

"I surely do, Cassy. I haven't had a decent meal in a fortnight."

"Well, just sit down at our table, Mister Dillard. I have a pot of rabbit stew warming, and there's a fresh made batch of biscuits." She smiled at him and went to the stove. "I swear, Boone, I just knew you were coming home today. It was like an angel told me." She laughed joyously. "And it told me to have some food ready, 'cause you'd be hungry as a bear comin' out of it's cave in springtime."

Boone smiled and settled in at the table. "Do we have any of that corn liquor left, darlin'? I surely could use a drink."

"Right there on the table in front of you," Cassy said. "In the pitcher with the grasshopper on it. That's always been my favorite piece of yours, and I filled it with the last of the corn mash."

Boone reached out for the pitcher and held it in his hands.

He looked lovingly at it as his fingers traced the shape of the grasshopper sitting on a blade of grass. "I *am* proud of this piece," he said. He poured a hefty draught of the homebrew into a matching mug, and then sipped at it slowly. "I sold my wares, Cassy. And I bought you some fine bolts of Chinese cloth," he said as his eyes became heavy with sleep. "They were red and blue and yellow with more things woven into them than I ever seen on any piece of cloth before. They had trees and flowers and birds and people. There were little towers, what they call pagodas, and ships and mountains and I don't know what all. But the soldiers took 'em from me. Said I was a looter." Boone's voice grew husky and his words slowed with each sip of the clear liquor. "But I paid for those bolts of cloth with my own money. I wanted so much for you to make some dresses for yourself. You'd 'a looked so beautiful wearin' 'em."

Cassy brought to the table one of Boone's yellow-ware plates, piled high with rabbit stew and biscuits. "Why, Boone, what on earth would I do with fancy China-cloth dresses? I don't need that kind of thing." She laughed again and it seemed to Boone as if a handful of song sparrows had flown into the room. "Can you just see me wearin' something like that whilst I tend to my chickens?" And the little sparrows chirped and fluttered around Cassy's head.

Boone smiled at his wife. "Well, I just wanted you to have somethin' nice. Somethin' to show my love for you."

"I know you love me, Boone. You're *here*, for Lord's sake. Now eat up before it gets cold." She poured another draft of corn liquor into Boone's mug. "I'm glad we had some left. I thought those Yankees had done drunk it all."

"What Yankees?" Boone asked.

"I'll tell you later, my love. Now I just want you to eat. In your own home, eat your dinner, made by your wife, who loves you with all her soul. Who shall love you for all eternity."

Boone fell to the rabbit stew with gusto, but after his arduous trek, the corn liquor quickly laid a sleepy hold on him. "How are the boys?" he asked through a mouthful of stew.

"They're just fine, my love. They're sleepin' the untroubled sleep of children. Oh my, will they be happy to see you in the mornin'." Standing behind Boone, Cassy's fingers tousled his hair as he ate. "They miss their father almost as much as I missed him."

"And Grandma?"

"She's fine, too."

"Did Jebber come home?"

Cassy shook her head, staring sadly into the dying embers within the belly of the stove. "We ain't seen Jebber nor Jewel for some time now."

Boone turned to look at Cassy. "You mean Jewel's gone, too?"

Cassy's eyes glazed with sorrow. "Somethin' bad happened to her and she had to leave. She was so ashamed."

Boone touched her arm. "What happened, Cassy?"

Cassy raised her head to the heavens and sighed deeply. "Those Yankees, Boone. That's what happened."

"But what did…?"

Before Boone could continue, Cassy bent down to kiss him on the lips to silence him. "No more questions, my love. Just finish your stew and warm your innards. She smiled the light of the sun once again. "Then I want you to take me to bed."

Boone nodded and turned back to his meal. He dipped half a buttermilk biscuit into the stew, popped it into his mouth, took a healthy pull on his mug of corn liquor to wash it down, and contentedly swallowed the lot. Then, feeling utterly spent, his shoulders slumped and his head bobbed. He barely moved the yellow-ware plate aside as his head tilted forward, face down onto the table, and he fell into a deep sleep of exhaustion.

Cassy's hands rubbed his back as she smiled at her man. She took off her shawl and draped it over Boone shoulders. After clearing the table of the plate and spoon, Cassy returned to Boone, kissed him on the top of his head, and whispered, "I will always be here for you, my love. You are the sun, and you are my light." She blew out the candle on the table and the room was plunged into darkness.

FIFTY-ONE

Boone felt something poking him in the back. Hard and insistent. And from out of his deep sleep he heard the words, "Git up, mister." Then another poke, and another. As he came up to consciousness, he thought for an instant that he was back at Meadow Wood, being poked by the stick of the Rebel corporal. But when he heard the voice again—"I said, wake up, you!"—he realized it was a woman's voice. And it wasn't Cassy's.

He lifted his head from the table and turned slowly in his chair to face the owner of the raspy voice. "My Lord, Boone!" it said. And there stood Delilah, with a shotgun in hand pointed square at Boone's chest.

"Grandma," Boone said as he rubbed the sleep from his eyes. "You don't have to shoot me. I ain't no thief or nothin'." He stretched out his arms to her and smiled.

Delilah dropped the shotgun to the floor and threw herself upon her grandson. "Oh, my dear, sweet child," she said as she clasped him to her bosom. "You're alive!" She wept tears of relief. "Your boys will be so happy. At least they will have their father now."

Boone held his grandmother to him, relieved to be home again and free of the obsession that had almost stolen his soul. Then her words registered with understanding. "But Nana, they have their mother, too. They'll have *both* of us now." He pulled free from Delilah and rose to his feet, stretching himself in the morning light. "Surely does feel good to be home, Grandma. And Cassy said she knew I was comin' last night. God, I love that woman. I never knew how much." He looked Delilah in the eyes. "But to tell the truth, I know now."

Delilah took a step back from him, a look of disbelief drawn across her face. "Boone, did you talk to Cassy last night?"

"I surely did. She'd fixed rabbit stew and biscuits for me 'cause she swore she knew I was comin.'" He smiled like the sun. "I guess she's startin' on that Dillard second sight, too, ehh, Nana?"

Delilah held her blank stare. "You talked to Cassy?"

"I reckon I did," he said. "An' I think I finished the last of the corn liquor, too. 'Cause Cassy said somethin' about Yankees drinkin' up nearly all of what we had. But there was just enough for me. Just enough to give me the good sleep I needed." He scratched his head with both his hands and yawned. "You know anythin' 'bout them Yanks she was talkin' of?"

Delilah put her hands to her cheeks and slowly shook her head. "Oh, my Lord," she said softly. "I want you to come with me, Boone."

"Outside?" Boone asked. "Nana, I want to see the boys first. An' I want to wake Cassy and have breakfast with my family. It can wait till after we eat, can't it?"

Boone turned and went toward the little room where the boys slept. He looked in and called to his oldest son. "Chap, I'm home." But the room was empty. He turned back to Delilah. "Where's the boys? With Cassy?"

"They ain't with Cassy," Delilah said.

Boone moved to the bedroom he shared with his wife. "Cassy?" he said as he opened the door.

"The boys are over at Jewel's house," Delilah said to Boone's back. "The three of us stay over there."

Boone looked into the empty bedroom. "Cassy?" he said again. Then he turned to Delilah. "Where *is* everybody?"

"I just told you, Boone."

He was confused. "Why y'all stayin' over there?"

Delilah swallowed back a tear. "I just couldn't stay here. Not after them Yankees. And when Jewel left…"

"Ain't she at home with Jebber?" Boone asked.

"They're both gone."

"Oh, yeah," Boone said, remembering Cassy's words. He shook his head. "Oh, Lordy, what a waste. And he did it all for her."

"What did Jebber do, son?"

"That's a long story for another time, Grandma. Let's go get Cassy and the boys." Boone took Delilah's arm and swept her to the front door. Then he stopped. "Get your shotgun, there, Nana.

Just stand it in the corner, 'cause you ain't gonna be needin' it no more. I'm home now." Boone laughed with a heartiness that almost washed away Delilah's sadness.

They stepped out into the summer morning of Coker Creek Hollow, and it was everything Boone remembered. Green and lush with a sweetness to the air and a soft breeze dissipating the morning mist. Boone looked about, smiling. "You know, Nana, this is just about the most beautiful little piece of land I have ever seen." He stared up into the sky, at the high, blue canopy overhead dappled with puffs of white clouds, the golden sun coming over the rise to the east, and he came back to himself. Back to his understanding of the earth. Back to his knowledge of growing things. Back to his love of the simplicity of life and the fine and good and eternal things life held. In other words, back to reality.

Boone spread his arms wide, as if to encompass his little valley, and he took a deep breath of the sweet morning air. "I do believe this is almost paradise," he said. His heart filled with a great ecstasy, for Boone knew, once again, that he was alive. Truly alive. And he was home. "Come on, Nana, let's get to my family."

He strode toward Jebber's house, but Delilah stopped him with a shout. "Wait, Boone! I must show you something first."

"What is it, Grandma? I don't like that sound in your voice."

She gently took his hand. "Come up the hill with me, Boone." Her voice now soft and comforting. "Everything will be all right."

They walked up a small hill to a mound of earth with a cross at the head of it, set under a gnarled, black hickory tree.

"My Lord," Boone said. "Who has died?"

"You go and look at the marker, son. I'll leave you alone here whilst I go to Jebber's house." Delilah quickly moved away from him, down the hill.

Boone stepped hesitantly to the grave, afraid of what the words on the cross would say. He moved beneath the branches of the black hickory, knelt beside the mound, and his worst fears were realized. The wood plaque on the cross of twisted dogwood read:

Cassandra Dillard
Wife and Mother
She is with the Angels

Boone cried out to the heavens, "No! Please, God, no!" He fell upon the mound, weeping. In his heart he knew it was Cassy, and he knew his life would never be the same without her. He wept with the tears of a man who had lost the most precious thing in his life. And he wept for his own folly and with the knowledge that the grave he was lying upon was the fruit of that folly.

He slowly sat up and spoke to the morning air. "I will always love you, Cassy. Forgive me for what I have done." A puff of breeze moved through the leaves over his head, rustling them as if in response to his words. As if in forgiveness of him. Boone looked up. "Thank you, my love," he said to the limbs of the tree. "And thank you for being there for me last night." He closed his eyes in remembrance. "You will always be with me, won't you?"

Before the wind in the tree could respond, a child's shout carried up from the glen below. "Daddy!" the voice cried out. "Daddy, you're home!" Boone turned to look and there was his son Chap, bursting ahead of Delilah, who held the baby in her arms. Chap was running for all he was worth and shouting at the top of his lungs, *"Daddy!"*

Boone stood and waved to his boy. "Chap! I'm here, son. I'm here!" Like a cannonball, Chap came rushing up the little hill and hurled himself into his father. Boone laughed and cried and spun around with his son in his arms.

"Oh, Daddy," Chap said, clinging to his whirling father. "I have *so* missed you!"

"I've missed *you*, son. But I'm home now," Boone said as he came to a stop from his spinning. "And I will never leave you again."

Chap clung to his father with all his strength. "I love you, Daddy." He laughed with a child's glee, but then grew somber. "Mom's dead," he said. "The Yankees shot her. They tried to kill us both when we was runnin' for the woods but I got away. The woods saved me."

Boone squeezed his son. "I surely am happy for that, Chap. You was always fast on your feet." Before Boone could say another word, Delilah was up to them with the baby cradled close.

"Look what I got here for you, Boone. Look at the size of this one," she said as she passed the baby to his father.

Boone took the boy from Delilah and hefted the toddler in the air. "Lord, this is gonna be a big one," he said. "Grandma, we're gonna have to get us a few more animals to feed these two. They might just turn out to be giants. Maybe even bigger than Jebber."

"We named him Matthew," Chap said excitedly. "Mom wanted that, or Luke. So I chose Matthew. An' we dipped him in the river and Grandma held him up to the sun an' said, 'This here is your new boy, Matthew Dillard.'"

"Just like that?" Boone said.

"Yep, just like she was talkin' to the sun itself."

Delilah smiled. "I *was* talkin' to the sun. But Chap, I was also talkin' to your ma. 'Cause that's where she is. In the sun."

"But she's right here," Chap said, pointing at the grave. "We put her in ourselves."

"That's only her body, boy," Delilah said. "She's everywhere, now. Her spirit's in *all* the light."

Boone laid a hand on Chap's shoulder. "An' I know she's in this ol' hickory tree. She spoke to me just before you came up."

Chap's eyes grew wide. "What did she say?"

"Oh, she was laughin' with happiness, Chap. Ya know what she sounded like? Like the wind blowin' through the leaves. And then she sounded like the birds, chirpin' in the branches."

Boone sat down next to Cassy's grave, comforting little Matthew in his arms. "Why don't we all sit down here with Mother and spend a little time with her. I know she'd like that."

Chap plopped himself down next to his father, and Delilah sat gently on the lush grass next to the mound. "Let's listen and see if we can hear her talkin' to us through the things what's around us," Boone said.

They all sat in silence, listening to the sounds of the earth swirling through Coker Creek Hollow. It seemed to Boone as if those sounds created a music of themselves. A music of simplicity, of the simple act of being alive. This must be the music of the angels, he thought to himself. He whispered to Delilah, "This is what the quiet peace of Heaven sounds like."

She smiled to her grandson. "It's Cassy," she said softly, "makin' a heaven for us here on the land. She'll be able to watch everything we do from up here."

"That will make her happy," Boone said. "Watchin' her children grow to men."

Then Chap cried out, "I hear her, Pa! Listen!"

Boone leaned forward. "Where, Chap?"

"Listen. Out there." He pointed to the farm buildings. "Hear her? She's in with the chickens. Can you hear her laugh mixin' with the chicken talk?"

Boone was silent for a moment, listening hard. "Why, I believe I can, Chap. Listen, Grandma."

They all went silent again, looking at Cassy's chicken coop as time slowed itself to its proper, unhurried pace, moving into late summer, in the Great Smokey Mountains of Tennessee, in the year of our Lord, 1863. The sun crested the eastern hills and shed its light full upon the Dillard farm in Coker Creek Hollow. And the little family, next to the grave of Cassy Dillard beneath the limbs of an old, black hickory tree, felt its warmth touch their faces. They were embraced by that warmth, enfolded by the rays of the sun. In peace.

And then a call came from off in the distance. "Halloo! Where is everybody?" And as the fates would have it, from around the barn, dressed in his Confederate officer's finery, came Jebber, riding atop his white horse with Jewel behind him, arms circled about his waist. They were laughing and shouting. "Ain't nobody here?" Jebber cried out.

"Chap! Delilah!" called Jewel. "It's me and Jebber. We're home!"

Chap jumped to his feet and shouted to the pair on horseback. "Hey! We're all up here!" Then he broke into a run, waving and calling to Jebber and Jewel. "Come on here! My pa's home!"

Jebber saw Chap, and then Boone and Delilah under the tree. "Hoo-whee!" he cried out. "Here we is! Home at last!"

Boone rose to his feet with little Matthew tucked close to his chest. He held a hand out to Delilah. "They're safe, Nana."

She took his hand and pulled herself up. "We're all safe now," she said.

Boone smiled at his farm and the sight of his boy racing down the green hillside to Jebber and Jewel. "The Lord has protected us," he said softly to Delilah.

The old woman looked up into the eyes of her grandson. "Or maybe it was Cassy," she said.

The soft morning breeze rustled the leaves of the hickory tree as the sparrows sang out their delicate song and the chickens in the henhouse clucked busily. Cassy's laughter could be heard everywhere in Coker Creek Hollow.

And it was almost paradise.

AFTERWORD

BY RICK VALENTINE

Ray Manzarek and I began a creative association in 1993 when he optioned for production my screenplay of Mikhail Bulgakov's cult classic of Russian magical realism, *The Master and Margarita*. We worked every angle to try to bring to the screen what we both considered to be a natural. It wasn't to be. Even Roman Polanski couldn't get his version off the ground some five to ten years before our assault on the castle.

So, at the turn of the century, Ray made his feature film directorial debut with "Love Her Madly," a low budget erotic thriller within a genre we christened Hip-Hop Hitchcock, which I scripted and co-produced. And between the little one we made and the big one that got away, arose *Snake Moon*. It is a story of misguided ambition, forbidden passion and an unbridled obsession which threatens to destroy the sanctity of familial bliss in a Edenic setting. Ray and I shared weekly story conferences, joined by our friend and producer Rick Schmidlin, and *Snake Moon* unfolded it's wings and flew as a Southern gothic tale of the supernatural set during the War Between the States. I began drafting the screenplay, and when the final fade was in place, Ray and I had in our collective grasp exactly what we had longed for; a haunting, morally probing tale...which unfortunately came to market just about the time that *Cold Mountain* ended the salability of Civil War screenplays.

But Ray felt the story and script were far too good not to be realized in some form: "I'm going to adapt *Snake Moon* into a novel," he said. And so he did, putting his spin on a masterful integration and profound elaboration of *Snake Moon's* film format. Interweaving both his words and mine, the result is a true collaboration between two friends with a shared vision. We hope you found our narrative to be revealing of certain yearnings and flaws endemic to the human condition, and a good page turning read.

Rick Valentine
March, 2006